YAMRAJ NUMBER 5003

Mrinal Chatterjee (born 1961), well known writer of offbeat fiction—novels and short stories—worked as a journalist for more than a decade before joining the Indian Institute of Mass Communication (IIMC; Eastern Regional Campus at Dhenkanal, Odisha) where he currently serves as the regional director and professor. Besides fiction, he has published works on journalism and mass communication; he also writes plays for stage and radio, and screenplays for television serials.

Thirumoy Banerjee (born 1987) completed his graduation in English literature from Calcutta University and is a journalist with a passion for reading and writing. He has worked with leading newspapers like *The Telegraph*, *The Indian Express* and *The Times of India*. He loves travelling and is an avid listener of Indian folk music.

YAMRAJ NUMBER 5003

Mrinal Chatterjee

Translated by
Thirumoy Banerjee

RUPA

Published by
Rupa Publications India Pvt. Ltd 2018
7/16, Ansari Road, Daryaganj
New Delhi 110002

Sales centres:
Allahabad Bengaluru Chennai
Hyderabad Jaipur Kathmandu
Kolkata Mumbai

ISBN: 978-81-291-5108-7

First impression 2018

10 9 8 7 6 5 4 3 2 1

The moral right of the author has been asserted.

Printed at Repro Knowledgecast Limited, Thane

Contents

Here is How It Began...

Reading newspapers is a good habit. It can make you an informed person, or you can rightfully boast to be one. Why only reading, even browsing through a newspaper is also a good habit to nurture. For instance, it can give you an idea to write a novel, as it happened in my case.

One lazy morning, I was browsing through the newspaper and saw this advertisement of the Indian Railways urging people not to cross level crossings, ignoring the safety instructions. In fact, some people are in such tearing hurry to cross level crossings that even if there is an iron pole obstructing their way, they will crawl from underneath that pole. In this particular advertisement, there was a picture of Yamraj near the level crossing sitting atop his *bahan*—the big black buffalo. The message was loud and clear: take care while crossing the level crossing, otherwise you may lose your life.

I recall I did not have much work on that day. Writers are

not supposed to work too hard. However, they are supposed to think hard. So I thought about Yamraj. Yamraj is supposed to take the spirits of the dead to Mrityuloka. If this Yamraj is waiting at this level crossing, how could the spirit of persons dying at this very hour be taken to Mrityuloka? Who would do that? How could one Yamraj do all the work? And why should he do this rather unpleasant work alone? There are so many Gods and Goddesses. Why couldn't others do it? I told you, I didn't have much work on that day. Fortunately, my wife was not around too. She was at her parents'. I believe that this kind of isolation is quite important for writers from time to time, and so it was for me. I began to think hard about the question that had come to my mind. The more I thought about it, the more I was intrigued by the character of Yamraj. I decided to read more about him. The more I read, the more I was fascinated by this character, its evolution and the various transformations it had had. I found that it is not a one-dimensional character. There are several layers to it. There are several angles and subtleties. If we go by the Puranas, there have been several ups and downs in the kind of tasks he has been assigned from time to time. From a position of high power to being reduced to a mere carrier—he has, probably, experienced much. By evening, I discovered a faint outline of a story emerging with Yamraj as the central character. I could almost feel somebody (was it Yamraj himself!) nudging me to write the story down. A seed of a story somewhere down in my mind was trying to germinate into a tiny sapling. I could feel the yearning and let it grow. And the seed did grow into two tiny, bright scarlet–green leaves, fluttering, like a baby waving its tiny palms. It grew to a plant, then a tree. It took about a month to write this novel. In this one month, I virtually inhabited the character of Yamraj, the protagonist of my story. My wife, who had by that time returned from her parents' place did not obviously like that. But I was too engrossed in living the life of my Yamraj to even care.

All seeds do not have a tree within it. Some do. Fewer still get an opportunity to grow into their full potential. I do not know whether this one grew to its full potential or not. Probably not, since potential should not have a full stop.

I enjoyed writing this rather slim novel. It was written in Odia and was published on my forty-ninth birthday in 2010. My mother and wife were mighty unhappy about the date of its release: why should you release a book on Yamraj on your birthday? I got an opportunity to deliver a small lecture and told them that every birthday is one step closer to one's day of death. So in a way, it is also a celebration of the end to come. Therefore, it should be celebrated with the release of a novel on Yamraj, the Lord of Death. They were not very impressed with my little lecture.

The book did well and was talked about in the literary circle. It was translated into Assamese by my (namesake) student Mrinal Nath. I wanted this to be translated into English so that it could reach a wider audience, but was a little apprehensive—would the readers understand and appreciate the nuances and references to our Puranas and ancient scriptures in English? Thirumoy Banerjee, a student of mine, persisted and finished the translation. And that was that.

Like every person, every book probably has a fate, of course linked to its karma. The English translation of the book was probably destined to be published now— eight years after the original in Odia was published. So it has. I'll be happy if you enjoy this book. And I know, Yamraj 5003 would be happy too, if he ever comes to know that you have read his story.

One last word: I must thank Shambhu (Sahu), again a former student of mine (see the advantage of being a teacher?), for taking this book up for publication, and Rinita (Banerjee) for her excellent copyediting.

Mrinal Chatterjee
23 December 2017

one

Yamraj at Bharatpur Level Crossing

The road joining Bharatpur and Nibaranpur has a level crossing at a short distance from the Bharatpur railway station. The railway lines join the north and the south while the road crosses it in the middle. Over the last couple of years, a level crossing has been constructed at the point where the tracks meet the road. A railway guard has also found a place at the crossing. Whenever a train is due to arrive, the gate is closed and a bell rings to ensure everyone is on alert. Once the gate is lowered, everyone is supposed to stop at the gate. But the cyclists and motorists find their way through. Despite the guard's repeated requests, there has been no stopping them. After all, they are the busiest people on earth.

Initially, there was no level crossing at this place. After

people turned it into a suicide zone and with many accidents being reported from here, locals started staging protests. Finally, a level crossing was constructed. People, however, continue to be careless. It is as if a delay of a couple of minutes will change their lives.

At this railway crossing, stood Yamraj 5003.

You must be asking: 'Yamraj is the Yamraj—Lord of Mrityuloka, the abode of the dead. How can he bear a number—is he some motor car or a prisoner?'

Before moving on, let me first clarify one thing. The common perception is that there is only one Yamraj—who moves on his buffalo with a thick rope in one hand and a mace in the other—who comes to take away the souls of the dead. The second part of the perception is correct, but there is not just one Yamraj. There are many. In this age of ever-increasing population, how can you expect *one* Yamraj to do all the work? Human population alone has crossed 600 crore. To add to that, there are birds, animals, insects and other creatures. The scriptures say that there are eighty-four lakh *yonis*—types of bodies or species—in the world. When any member of any yoni dies, Yamraj is supposed to come to take away its soul. Is it possible for a single Yamraj to do so much work?

Obviously not!

And the work does not end with just taking the soul away; he has to decide its future—like if it will go to heaven or hell. Chitragupta is just a clerk! He only keeps a track of the deeds of men. After the soul reaches Yamraj, Chitragupta just hands him the accounts of people's deeds. Yamraj decides its future—if it will take birth again, go to heaven or hell, and if it stays in hell, which of the twenty-one hells it will inhabit. What will be its punishment? Just imagine the amount of time it can take one person to take all these decisions. In the world, it takes ages to deliver a judgement even on trivial issues. And this is the question of an entire life!

So the fact remains that in Mrityuloka, there are many identical Yamrajs. Now, how did that happen? The answer is simple: Yamraj has been cloned. The process of manufacturing an identical person from an individual is referred to as 'cloning'. You must have read the story of the cloning of a sheep, Dolly. Then dogs have been cloned, cows have been cloned. A few years ago, a South Korean scientist claimed that he could even clone human beings. The whole world is now busy debating if human beings should be cloned. But in Devaloka, the process of cloning has been happening for thousands of years. I am sure you remember the story of Ma Kali and Raktabija. The ones who have forgotten that story amid their busy schedules, I shall assist you in recollecting.

Thousands of years ago, a demon—following hard penance and meditation—got a boon that from each drop of his blood, a new demon will be formed. Thus, he was named Raktabija (*rakta* means blood and *bij* means seed). Just like a tree is born from a seed, a complete new demon will be born from just a drop of blood. After getting this boon, he became very arrogant and created havoc in Triloka. The Gods could not figure out how to destroy him. They went to Vishnu. Vishnu sought Parvati's help. Parvati obliged. She transformed herself into Kali to destroy Raktabija. She held a scimitar and every time she beheaded Raktabija, a new demon would be cast from every drop of his blood. She became tired after a while. She could not get the better of Raktabija. The battle raged on.

Then an idea came to her mind. These days it is said that an idea can change the way of life. Here, it became a legend. 'Only when a drop of his blood falls on the ground would a new demon be born,' she thought.

She started beheading Raktabija and his clones, collected the blood oozing in a bowl and drank it. As blood could not touch the soil, no more identical demons could take birth and Raktabija was finally destroyed.

Remember Ma Kali's picture? If you cannot remember that too, you can open your *panji*. All panjis contain pictures of Gods and Goddesses; you would surely find her. Four-armed Ma Kali holds a scimitar with her upper right hand, the severed head of a demon with her upper left hand and the bowl with the lower left hand to contain the drops of blood from the severed head. The head is Raktabija's.

Now, forget the story. Think about the phenomenon of the creation of a new demon from a single drop of blood.

What is it?

Cloning!

Same was the case with Ravan. Going with the Ramayana, Ravan had ten heads. You behead one and the other comes out. What do you think that is?

Cloning!

The art of creating an entire being out of a single cell was known to our Gods and Goddesses.

Using the cells of the main Yamraj, many other Yamrajs have been created. According to the Rig Veda, when the first man went to Mrityuloka, he was made its lord. He was the first Yamraj. The Rig Veda, however, does not mention that Brahma, the creator of the holy Trinity, used that one Yamraj to create many others.

How can these things be written? The truth of the matter is that Brahma did not just create other Yamrajs. He brought about some changes in each of them. Each batch of Yamrajs had some distinct qualities in terms of their physique and nature—just like it happens in modern genetic engineering. There are a number of modifications done to flowers and fruits; likewise, there were modifications made in the Yamrajs too.

There is enough proof for this.

The picture of Yamraj that we get in the Rig Veda is that of a light-tempered person, who was made the master of Mrityuloka and was asked to decide the norms and rules under which the spirits of the deceased would have to live there.

Now, let's see the description of Yamraj in the Upanishads. It is mainly of that of a teacher. There, Yamraj emphasized on truth and the achievement of divinity. However, later, there have been a number of changes applied to his nature, appearance and also his character. He has become more and more frightening. The colour of his body has transformed itself to green. He has started sporting a thick moustache and has a gigantic body. His behaviour has also become more and more rough as the centuries have passed. These changes have been brought about in him willingly by the Trinity—Brahma, Vishnu and Maheshwar. They did it to maintain some decorum not only in the world but also beyond it. The concept of death as something fearsome has been created, to instil fear into the minds of all human beings besides other creatures. This is precisely why Yamraj has been transformed into such a fearful, almost scary figure.

Yamraj has many names: Dharmaraj, Yama, Dharma, Pritipeti, Bibhatswa and Mrityu. Observe the names closely. You will get a hint of the altered attitude in him. But the change was brought about so slowly and deftly that nobody had the chance to comprehend it. This has continued ever since. As the number of creatures in the world is increasing, more Yamrajs are being created. Since all the Yamrajs look relatively alike, everyone thinks that the Yamraj is a single entity.

There is a class division among the Yamraj clones as well. Just as there is a queen bee that all the bees are servants to, there is one chief Yamraj. He looks like the other Yamraj clones, but his brain has been created in a special way. His main work is to punish or reward the souls that reach Mrityuloka, while the rest do other sundry work, like bringing the souls from the earth to Mrityuloka, punish the sinners, look after the administration of hell, etc. Not just Yamraj, his companion buffalo and the dogs have also been cloned.

All of them look alike. There is a similarity between all the Yamrajs and their companions. Only Yamraj 5003 has become slightly different from the rest.

The difference does not lie in how he looks or his structure—the difference lies in his behaviour. His behaviour and mental make-up is different from others'.

How this happened is an interesting story.

What happened was while Brahma was busy cloning Yamraj 5003, Saraswati called him. That day, Mrityuloka needed a number of Yamrajs. If there is extra pressure at work, don't we need more hands? It is no different in heaven. Each time there is a natural calamity—floods, cyclones, drought or some epidemic—the requirement of Yamrajs goes up proportionately.

Today, the number of wars has reduced, but terrorism has increased multifold. Every other day there are terrorist strikes in some corner of the world—at times on trains, at others in buses, or hotels. Attacks at various religious places have made news several times in the last few years.

New diseases are coming to the fore, many of which are often leading to epidemics like Zika, bird flu, Ebola. And who can forget the swine flu? The whole world went crazy at the outbreak of this epidemic.

Under such circumstances, Brahma has to create Yamrajs in a hurry. He does not involve anyone else in this work, but chooses to do everything on his own. As said before, the day Yamraj 5003 was being created, the demand was very high. Brahma was busy cloning Yamraj 5003, when suddenly Saraswati called him.

Brahma loves Saraswati dearly. When a beloved calls, one is bound to respond. In this regard, there isn't any difference between man and God. Brahma left Yamraj 5003 in the cloning machine and went to meet her.

You can call Saraswati Brahma's daughter as well as his wife. As the scriptures say, he created Saraswati and later accepted her as his wife. Therefore, she gets the love of both daughter and wife from Brahma.

The highly intellectual Saraswati played a major role in creating the universe. Without her help, Brahma would certainly have found it difficult to do the work on his own. She also played a major role in the creation of language and script. Sanskrit is her creation. She has a special inclination towards poetry. In case of language and literature, Brahma fully depends on her.

Brahma had been contemplating a change in the structure of the brains of poets. In this connection, he had asked Saraswati to conduct a study. Saraswati had gathered some facts and she wanted to hand them over to Brahma. Their conversation was long; therefore, Brahma took quite some time to return.

At this point Narad reached Brahmaloka. Let alone men, it is difficult even for Gods to reach this place. Naturally, the cloning compartment is a place not visited by anyone. But Narad is not 'anyone'. Neither is he an ordinary God. In *Srimad Bhagwat Mahapurana*, he has been referred to as an 'avatar'. He is also Brahma's *manas santan*. Brahma had taken special care to teach him music.

Saraswati's favourite, veena, is his creation. Being Brahma's favourite, Narad freely moves throughout the Brahmaloka. Now, Brahmaloka's security person said, 'Prajapita Brahma was in the cloning room; he just left for home now.' Thinking that it would not be right to go to Brahma's place at such an odd time, Narad went into the cloning room.

After entering the room, he saw a 'Yamraj' inside the cloning machine, a sheet of paper pinned on his chest stating that he was 'Yamraj number 5003'.

That Yamrajs are cloned is a known fact to everyone in heaven, so this didn't give rise to any curiosity in him. Suddenly, he saw the body of a man on another table. In Yamraj's cloning room, bodies of human beings never come. There are separate rooms for creating human beings.

This particular room is exclusively for creating Yamrajs. Why has the corpse of a mortal made its way into this room?

Narad's inquisitive mind failed to comprehend this. He went close to the table. A number of wires were attached to the head of the man. The wires were attached to a big machine that can read into the workings of the human brain. Narad had some idea about the machine. The identity written on the table of the man stated that he was a poet, recently brought into this place.

Why has the body of a poet been brought here? Narad started asking himself. He felt like asking Brahma about it. So, he began to wait for him and went close to the body.

'A handsome body lying lifeless. Without the wires, it would have been very difficult to understand if the man was dead or alive,' Narad thought.

At this point, a stray thought entered Narad's fertile mind: what would happen if Yamraj, the King of Mrityuloka, had the brain of a poet? Would the poet's brain impact Yamraj's nature? Would it be altered in any manner?

A poet is soft-hearted, Yamraj is supposed to be the opposite. Poets are emotional, Yamraj is rational. If the brain cells of the poet are put in the Yamraj's brain, would there be a change in Yamraj's attitude and behaviour?

Narad has it in his nature—when something enters his mind, he remains impatient till he has an answer or finds a solution. Naturally, he became fidgety and curious after seeing the body of a poet inside the cloning room exclusively for creating Yamrajs.

Brahma's not coming either.

His anxiety started getting the better of him. He had some ideas about the formation of the human brain. He knew which brain cells controlled the behaviour of men. He wanted to see what happens when... He started pacing the room. But how long can a man keep walking up and down the room!

He inserted some brain cells of the poet into Yamraj 5003's brain.

The cells that Narad inserted into Yamraj's brain, belonged to a young romantic poet of Odisha, who had died of a heart attack. This was preceded by a break-up. Romantic poets are not only romantic, they are emotional as well. The poor poet could not take the shock. He started drinking heavily, like Devdas. There was no chance of survival, once he took to weed.

Chitragupta sent his body to Brahma.

This is not a commonality. Usually, one's body is delivered to heaven or hell after judging his actions during his lifetime.

Brahma had, for quite some time, been thinking of redesigning the Yamrajs' brains and therefore, for the sake of experimenting, he needed some bodies of poets. It was on Brahma's request that the body was sent to Brahmaloka.

Narad had acted on an impulse. Little did he know about the consequences.

After the brain cells of the poet entered Yamraj 5003's body, it started trembling. As the cells started getting absorbed, the shivering started getting more violent. Various types of expressions began to appear on his face. At one point, it seemed as if he was happy. The next moment it seemed as if he was screaming in extreme pain. Sometimes his eyes lit up as if experiencing a good feeling and in the very next moment his face turned into a sad sculpture and again it bore the expression of an anger-stricken individual. All the nine *rasa*s were visible on his face.

Seeing the condition and the changes in the Yamraj, Narad was shell-shocked. He realized that his intervention had been a blunder of sorts. He closed down all the machines attached to the Yamraj and the poet's body. He hoped that Brahma would not come to know about his deeds.

But Brahma is the creator, after all.

When Brahma entered the room, Narad was almost caught unawares.

He asked, 'Son, when did you come?'

'I...I...just a few minutes back,' Narad stuttered, 'I hadn't seen you for a long time, so...'

'Oh! Good that you came. Come, have a seat. Saraswati has prepared grape juice. Have some.'

'Oh! Not now. I've got to go.'

Narad's panic-stricken expressions and the change in the chords attached to Yamraj 5003 immediately drew Brahma's attention. It created some doubts in his mind. To clear his suspicion, he checked the readings of the machines attached to the poet's brain. He immediately understood what had gone wrong.

How could Narad lie to Brahma? Upon learning that cells from the poet's brain had been inserted into Yamraj's, Brahma became very impatient. Using all his four hands, he tried to extract the cells.

But some of the poet's cells had already fixed themselves into Yamraj's brain. It was impossible to remove them anymore.

Brahma became really tense now. Wrinkles started appearing on his forehead. With one hand he started scratching his long white beard while the three other hands were busy pressing the buttons attached to the body. He kept turning the knobs restlessly.

The scratching of the beard after experiencing anxiety is an old habit of Brahma's. Looking at his face, Narad became absolutely certain that he had committed a huge mistake.

Had this mistake been committed by anyone else, Brahma would have burnt him into ashes. But Narad was his manas santan. Moreover, according to Indian mythology, Narad is a highly educated man. Above all, he is a journalist. You can do anything to anyone, but you cannot harm a journalist—at best you may reprimand or scold him.

That Brahma did. He scolded Narad vehemently, and uttered words that he had never before. But all beginnings have ends. Scolding is a tough business. It is terribly exhausting. And, Brahma is ageing!

After a while Brahma felt exhausted.

When he paused to get his breath back, Narad knelt down and begged forgiveness.

'Prajapita, I have committed a huge mistake, a blunder. Please forgive me.'

Brahma observed that Narad's cheeks had turned red, his eyes had begun watering and the nose had swollen up. Journalists usually do not seek forgiveness. Seeing Narad's state, Brahma's heart melted. He said, 'What's done cannot be undone. But never mention this to anyone. I have done my best to control the damage, but a few cells from the poet remain in Yamraj's head. It won't be possible to remove them anymore. That the poet's nature has made its way into the Lord of Death should never be known. If Vishnu and

Maheshwar come to know about this, they will be furious. Of all the people who exist in the universe, poets are the only ones they fear. Poets are not practical, or logical. Neither are they rational. They don't even believe in hierarchy. They flout norms that have been set for mankind. They have rebellion in their blood. Seeing these characteristics, Vishnu and Maheshwar had asked me to re-engineer the poet's brain. That was precisely why he was brought here. And you idiot have inserted a revolutionary's cell into the head of Yamraj!'

Narad is a journalist—it is not in his nature to keep a secret. If anyone asks him not to disclose something, that piece of secret shall be the first thing he will spread. Until he does that, he feels suffocated, as if his heart will burst. It is because of this characteristic, that the clever Gods tell him only those things that they want others to know, to spread, always adding, 'Don't say this to anyone'. They know that in no time word shall spread everywhere.

But Narad understood the consequences of this action. He realized that if Vishnu and Maheshwar come to know about this, he will indeed be in trouble. His licence of moving around everywhere freely would be the first thing to go. And if there is no freedom to travel anywhere, how can he carry on with his job as a journalist?

To add to that, Maheshwar is an unpredictable God.

No one knows what he will do. If his third eye opens in anger, he might burn down everything! Everybody knows what happened to Kamadeva.

This thought sent a tremor down Narad's spine. 'No, I shall not talk about this incident to anybody. But even that might not help. There will be differences in the attitude and behaviour of Yamraj 5003. Everyone will come to know of the truth eventually.'

As Narad voiced his apprehensions, Brahma mulled over them for some time and then said, 'Leave that to me. Know this my son, the technique of keeping a secret is not to keep it as one. Say some part of a truth, not the whole of it. In this case, I shall say that while creating this Yamraj, there were some mechanical defects and hence the disparities. But *you* should never disclose the whole truth.'

'I will never say this to anyone. This goes down as the biggest mistake I have ever committed. I won't do such a thing ever again.'

After leaving Brahmaloka, Narad took out his *dhenki* and sat on it. He was still in a state of shock. He had never been insulted like this, neither had he felt so ashamed of something he did. Prajapita Brahma had called him a 'senseless fellow'.

He had also called him a bumbling idiot who interferes

in everything. He had said, 'So what, that you are Narad in this birth? The ill effects of your previous births have remained.'

When anyone talks about his previous birth, Narad becomes very angry. The deeds of his past life bring back memories of humiliation and enrage him.

Narad's history is very interesting. In the previous birth, Narad was Upavarhan, the lord of the Gandharvas. Once, the Gandharvas and the Kinners were singing devotional songs in the heart of Brahmaloka. In that sacred place, Upavarhan, proud of his good looks, misbehaved with the women present. Brahma became livid with him and cursed him to a life in a Shudra family. Thus, upon Brahma's curse, Narad was born in a Shudra family. However, it so happened that his mother was a pious lady who used to serve the Brahmins, and was well conversant in the Vedas. The good qualities of his mother shown themselves in Narad's behaviour. His mother was in the house of a Brahmin where these four yogis arrived in the four months of a rainy season. At that time, Narad's mother was asked to look after these yogis. Narad, then five years old, served them along with his mother, wholeheartedly. On the suggestion of the yogis, Narad started learning 'Bhagawat Keertan'. Following the four months, when the yogis were preparing to leave, Narad expressed his desire to go with them. The yogis said, 'Son, at this point, it is your duty to serve your mother.' But soon after, Narad's mother died of a snakebite. The only emotional bond Narad had was gone—he became a lone man in a lonely world. The life that followed was one of hard penance. After death, his soul merged with Brahma's. Thereafter, he was recreated and Narad became a companion of the Trinity. But even after so many births, Narad still has to suffer the consequences of Gandharva Upavarhan's actions. Prajapita Brahma had said that traces of Upavarhan were still present in him, that he was a bumbling fool.

A fit of rage seized his heart. And in that reason-blinding fit of rage, Narad started thinking that all this had happened only because of Yamraj 5003. Had his body not been there at that point of time, would he have been able to insert the poet's brain cells into Yamraj's? Because of the body of that man, all this has happened. It was only because of that Yamraj that Narad, who is respected by all, who has accomplished so many great tasks, had to be humiliated and in such a manner. The more he thought of it all, the more enraged he became. Sandalwood cools the body, but can anything calm the heart?

As per the rules of the Brahmaloka, the defective clone was supposed to be destroyed. But since Brahma thought that the defect was not severe, he didn't do so. Everything was fine with Yamraj 5003, only that there were some weaknesses in his nature. While delivering Yamraj 5003 to Mrityuloka, Brahma asked to inform Chitragupta that this one had been made hastily and therefore, he was not going to be as 'efficient' as the rest. 'Don't assign him any difficult task,' Brahma had cautioned.

So, Yamraj 5003 was being given easy tasks. In the busy atmosphere of Yamloka, the poetic instincts remained embedded somewhere deep within his heart. They never had an opportunity to flower. Even if something happened, it went unnoticed. Everyone forgot that there were some defects in his brain.

Now let us go back to the Bharatpur railway crossing, where Yamraj 5003 is standing.

Standing would be an incorrect way of putting it; he was almost floating in the air. The common man cannot see such visions. Else everyone at the Bharatpur railway crossing would have seen that five to six feet above the ground, right on top of the level crossing, Yamraj was standing—exactly as one would normally see him in the pictures printed in panjis. Bare, green body; huge belly; moustache like a horse's tail; wearing a dark red silk dhoti, a golden chain around the neck, a thick bangle on the wrist, armlets, a crown; and holding a silver buttoned mace. He stands alongside his bahan—a big black buffalo—by his side. A leather rope was tied and hung around one of the horns of the buffalo, which had a bell attached to his neck. The rope is used to tie and drag the soul to Mrityuloka. The thick-necked buffalo was occasionally moving his head and tail from side to side. There was no reason for the thick-skinned buffalo to feel the presence of mosquitoes since he was not visible to the naked eye. But habit is habit. Buffaloes have the habit of moving their heads and tails. It is not in their nature to stand still.

Behind the buffalo, in safe distance, were seated two ferocious two-headed dogs, with four eyes each that could look in four directions. They are always present when Yamraj is out to fetch someone's soul. If any spirit refuses to come, these dogs drag them to hell. (This is the secret behind people's fear upon hearing a dog's wail. They think that Yamraj's dogs have come as they are the first ones to sense something. Dogs crying indicates Yamraj's presence, which means that someone will die soon. In Nepal, dogs are worshipped because of this. The Dark Moon cycle that comes after Durga Puja sees the Kukur (Dog) Tihar. 'Tihar', in their language, means 'festival'. On this day, all dogs, pets as well as street dogs, are worshipped and given good food and garlands, the objective being to appease Yamraj's dogs. The belief being that if they do so, they won't be dragged to hell.)

The worldly dogs, however, do not cry at Yamraj's dogs—they probably cry at the poor condition of the two-headed dogs of Mrityuloka! They must be wondering, who managed to add that second head? No relief even after death! These dogs have to work for Yamraj, as gatekeepers of hell.

Let me tell you now that according to the Puranas, there is the river Baitarani between this world and the next. If one crosses the river, he will come across two two-headed dogs. These are the gatekeepers of hell. To reach the land of death, one has to cross them.

Mortals are afraid of these two-headed dogs and these dogs, in turn, are afraid of the Yamraj's bahan.

Funny, ain't it?

In this world, everyone is afraid of someone or the other.

Yamraj's dogs have enough reasons to be afraid of the buffalo and to keep a safe distance from him. The buffalo has a habit of kicking. Men cannot see or feel its presence, but the inmates of hell can not only see them all the time, they are well accustomed to its behaviour as well. The dogs have been kicked by the buffalo in the past. Thus, whenever he is around, the dogs take extra care.

Behind the dogs, stand two yamdoots . Huge and broad, they are real fearsome figures. Like Yamraj, even they have a moustache similar to a horse's tail. In Mrityuloka, most yamdoots have moustaches of that kind. For yamdoots, sporting a moustache is not mandatory, but just a trend. Chitragupta says the moustache is the pride of yamdoots. If you don't have a moustache, what kind of a yamdoot are you?

Somehow, the moustache has become far too associated with the yamdoots. Even the administration of Yamloka wants to maintain this image. Thus, for sporting the moustache, these yamdoots get an incentive. For the moustache, they get two kilograms of mustard oil that everyone in Yamloka uses. This oil is produced by all the offenders who are going through the process of retribution. The sinners get different punishments. Producing oil through hard labour is one of them. If anyone is seen relaxing, they are whipped and forced to get back to their work. Therefore, there is no shortage of oil in Yamloka.

Yamdoots are not cloned like Yamrajs. None of the yamdoots are clones; in fact, they were human beings at one point in time. After arriving at Yamloka, they became yamdoots.

How one can become a yamdoot is also a story. This bit of information could be of some help for you. I know many of you might be thinking of being yamdoots yourselves. Honestly, becoming a yamdoot in the Mrityuloka is like becoming a software engineer or an IAS officer in India— much sought after.

First, let me explain to you the work of a yamdoot. *Doot*, in Hindi, means messenger, that is, someone who carries a message. Yamdoot implies carrying messages for Yamraj. You may snigger, 'How respectable is the job? It is rather petty.'

Here, let me tell you another thing. No work is big or small. However, power is great. The more visible and widespread the impact of the work, the more powerful the man becomes.

Look at the administrators and you'd know what I mean. What is their work? To administrate! After someone formulates a rule, they just operationalize it. But the impact of the decision is not limited! After all, their work impacts so many people—the fortunes of many depend on the decisions. Putting it frankly, if they want, they can harm many people and put them in trouble. The more people you harm, the more powerful you become and the more powerful you become, the more arrogance creeps into you.

Yamdoots are no different. They are smeared in pride— after all they work in the Mrityuloka, where all the residents are to undergo punishment for sins committed while they were alive. Yamdoots are their virtual masters. After passing the statement of punishment, Yamraj's work is over. Now it is up to the yamdoots to see how to carry out the orders, to meet the deadlines of the work. The cloned Yamrajs are supposed to supervise the work. But they do not visit the Mrityuloka frequently—they have more important things to do. So yamdoots virtually have the power to mete out as much punishment as they want—fifty whips to some or ten to others—as and when they like. If they want, they put some into burning oil or make them stand on the kiln. That is why people pray for mercy to them every day—a mercy that may help reduce the punishment they are to suffer and lessen their pain. Only a yamdoot knows what it is to be like one. Rulers of the world until yesterday—whom you could only see on television screens or in photographs in newspapers, under whom there were hundreds of servants, today have been turned into mere beggars. They are literally begging the yamdoots for mercy. When alive, they were on the top, today they are beneath a yamdoot's feet. The yamdoot can even kick one at will. The satisfaction of such acts is boundless.

This is the secret behind the wish for all those who want to be yamdoots after death. Apart from the sadistic pleasure of beating up the punished at will, there are other benefits of the post too. They can come to work at their own sweet time, they can have the best food available while they visit the earth to fetch the soul of a departed being. Not many know that the tasty worldly cuisines are not available in Mrityuloka. The food served in Mrityuloka is nutritious, but bland and tasteless. Therefore, many yamdoots eagerly look forward to get the opportunity to visit the earth.

Please note that it is not an easy job to bag the post of a yamdoot. Not everyone is fortunate enough to be a yamdoot. Having a massive physique is mandatory. The person should be blessed with a calmness of temper and should be able to endure a lot of pain himself. But above all, the yamdoot should be loyal to the master, he should carry out the orders diligently and be honest while doing so. Only after a candidate has met all these conditions, can he become eligible for the job.

If you are still unable to understand, let me tell you the system in Mrityuloka. It is a known fact that mortals commit a number of sins during their lifetime. But at the same time, another big truth is that the same mortals do things that are counted under the category of *punya* or good work. Now, there are different grades of sin. Stealing guava from someone else's garden is a sin, and murdering someone is also a sin—but there is a difference between the two. In Mrityuloka, such differences are considered before the punishment is meted out or a reward given. The person is accordingly sent to heaven or is retained in the clutches of hell. Often, a decision comes in the form of a tie. In such cases, the person is sent to the world—you are right, the person is sent to the world to be born again.

Before the final verdict, the punished is asked. 'Where do you want to go' is often the question. After he has communicated his request, the final verdict is given. Say someone has committed a small crime and conducted himself well—such a person is likely to become a yamdoot. He has to meet the other criteria, of course.

Previously, if someone became a yamdoot, he remained one for a lifetime. But that created several problems. Some yamdoots misused their powers—an inherent quality in human beings. Even after death, a faint impression of the human being's nature remains. The traces are found even after they are given the post of yamdoot in the Mrityuloka. To avoid this misuse, their tenures are fixed, after which some are sent to heaven, and some, to the world.

For ages, yamdoots have been enjoying a lot of power—but now the trend seems to be changing a little. The point is there is a fall in the population in hell as more and more people are going to heaven. You may ask how this is possible—the answer is simple.

People are becoming more and more religious, if not pious. Every roadside has a temple or a mosque or a church in India. Every day, new shrines spring up. Then, there is almost a tsunami of devotional songs—bhajans. From religious places to radio, television to local pan shops and even buses—all play bhajans. Bhajan programmes are often organized in public places. So you cannot help but listen to them. Scriptures say you earn punya by listening to bhajans.

It does not end there. It is written, that before death, chanting God's name will assure one a place in heaven. Today, every hospital has a temple. The way bhajans are played so loudly there, the heart patients are certain to die way early! And there are high chances that after their death, they would find themselves a place in heaven.

Moreover, the number of *baba*s is also on the rise—they spread their holy messages from city to city and also through television. Had it not been for the saas-bahu serials, these holy messages were sure to take many more to heaven.

So what if Chitragupta's work table now has a computer, the rules of Mrityuloka are old. If before death the name of God is chanted into the ears, the dying are sure to go to heaven. Going to heaven is suddenly so easy!

Once upon a time, so much effort was required for it. No longer. Just as each middle-class person can travel by air today, anyone can go to heaven as well.

With so many people reaching heaven, the position of heaven as the most sought after place is suddenly at stake. Devraj Indra has started discussing the matter with the Trinity.

Now, returning again to the spot of the incident. Yamdoot number 404 and 812 were accompanying Yamraj 5003. I have already told you that yamdoots are not clones. Neither do they look the same, nor are their characters the same—each one is different. Each one has a separate name and a distinct identity. But in the Mrityuloka, they are called by their numbers. There are reasons for this. There are lakhs of yamdoots. Each year so many yamdoots change that it is hardly possible to remember all the names. To remove the confusion, numbers have been assigned. The rule is that when a yamdoot retires, the newly appointed would have the same numbers as had been assigned to the predecessors.

The names of Yamdoot 404 and 812 are Habul and Babul, respectively—they call each other by their names. Yamraj 5003 also calls them by their names. Other Yamrajs do not put in that extra bit of effort to remember all the names. But Yamraj 5003 asks, 'Are they machines, that you will call them by their numbers? Names form their distinct identity. Would there be no difference between a machine and a yamdoot...?' Habul and Babul do not understand all this and neither do they think it necessary to do so. However, when someone calls them by their names, they feel good.

They realize that this Yamraj is a little different. They wished that all Yamrajs were like this. Yamraj 5003 is looked upon with a lot of admiration. He is always polite with everyone. Not only Habul or Babul, but everyone wants to go on duty with him.

Let me introduce you to yamdoots Habul and Babul before getting on with the story. Habul was a police constable after which he became a prison guard. Babul was a goon. Babul was sent to jail for two years where Habul was posted. Babul had a habit of drinking in the evening. If he did not get his drink after sundown, he would feel ill. Drinking was not allowed in prison. Babul felt he would die without his drink. Worried, Babul started crying, when Habul came as a godsend to enquire about the cause of his agony. Learning the cause, he made some arrangements. Habul knew that supplying liquor was one of the biggest services to mankind. Babul returned this extremely kind favour by coming to Habul's aid. In today's world one can do little with the meagre salary of a prison guard. Habul's son was not being able to get admission in an engineering college. Babul told Habul,

'Don't worry brother! What am I there for?' The next day, Babul got Habul ₹2 lakh and his job was done. By serving each other, they earned the benefit of having done 'good deeds'.

Both of them reached the Mrityuloka together.

It so happened that a riot broke out in jail. The inmates and the guards started fighting. Not all prisoners had the same kind of relation with the guards like Habul and Babul did. As a result of the riots, both these friends died and were brought to Yamloka. Considering their deeds and the past experience, they were given the posts of yamdoots.

They are a great duo. Their performance together as yamdoots has been commendable. They are always sent on duty together. Habul already has past experience of bringing people in and Babul has the experience of overpowering the unwilling ones with a punch or two. Because Yamraj 5003 has a different nature, Habul and Babul are sent with him in cases of urgency, so that they can be of help.

Every morning, Chitragupta switches his computer on and announces the upcoming deaths. Then different Yamrajs, accompanied by different yamdoots, are allotted the assignments of the day. Different states have been allotted to different Yamrajs. One set for Odisha, one for Andhra, another for Gujarat and so on. This is done to ensure least difficulty in locating the places. After the allotment of duties, each Yamraj goes to the respective places and their work is not over until they submit the souls they are supposed to bring from the earth to Chitragupta.

When Habul was alive, as a police constable, for several years he had done this job. The sole difference is that today he no longer has a transportation problem. People die at a specific time and the yamdoots bring the soul to Chitragupta. At times, some spirits act in a mischievous manner and they remain stuck to the body, for instance, the spirits of politicians. Due to the way these people get stuck to their positions, it often becomes very difficult to get hold of their spirits. Even Yamraj's two-headed dogs have to sweat it out to drag their spirits out. Once, something went terribly wrong. It so happened that they had come to take the soul of a political leader who had been a minister for a long time. Though he was quite old, he continued to be in active politics and was trying to win the elections. Chitragupta announced one morning that it was time for the leader to die and his soul was to be brought to Mrityuloka. That day it took the yamdoots longer than usual to reach the world. With so many satellites and rockets in space, the roads have become congested. They reached late and found that the body lay without the spirit! They looked around, but the spirit could not be located. If the spirit was not found, it would be a huge problem—the rules of nature would be in a mess, warned Chitragupta. Everybody was worried. The news reached Vishnu's ears; even he was disturbed. The search continued for long and finally it was discovered that the spirit was attached to his chair! Finally, with much effort, the spirit was brought to the Mrityuloka. Ever since, Habul and Babul look around the chairs of politicians after their death, lest they be attached there again!

Another category of people whose spirits give the Yamrajs a tough time are the ones in nursing homes. They are the old men and women who want to die, but the doctors become the reason for all the hassle. Patients almost dead are forcefully made to remain alive, as doctors insert pipes into all parts of their bodies, and with all the available injections obstinately ensure that these people remain alive. It often happens that even their children pray for their death. But they can never ask the doctor to stop treatment. How can they? Neither can they talk about the death of their parents nor can they accept them being alive in that manner. In many countries, there is a raging debate on mercy killing: a man who is bedridden for several years and for whom the chances of recovery are close to nil, or when the patient himself or herself wants to die, what is the point in forcibly keeping him alive? Under such circumstances, if euthanasia is implemented, the yamdoots' job becomes so much simpler! Whether a man who is in coma for years should be allowed to die or not is a debate going on for years now. But there is a counterargument: what if the man in coma suddenly recovers? What is impossible in today's world? Just think if a man wants to kill another in the name of mercy killing, then he achieves his evil motives a lot simply. Too many problems...

There are classifications of doctors as well. To keep it short, I place them into two categories. There is one category that actually wishes the betterment of the patient and has the good intention of curing him. And there is a second category—which is easier to find these days—of those who want the patient to be alive only for the sake of making a fast buck. Death of the patient is like the end of game for them. It's like those lawyers who never want the closure of a court case. The judge says, 'end the case'; the lawyer tells the client, 'you will win, just wait for the next hearing'.

In cases such as these, yamdoots have to stay idle and wait. And that is what they hate most—neither can they go anywhere, nor can they do anything concrete. As soon as the spirit leaves the body, it has to be taken to Chitragupta who hates even the slightest delay.

Habul and Babul were waiting with irritated faces. They were told that at 7.13 in the morning, a young lady will commit suicide at the Bharatpur railway crossing. Getting the spirit in cases of suicide is a little difficult—the slightest delay in catching the spirit and it turns into a ghost, which would mean that it will reach Mrityuloka years later. Many dissatisfied spirits want to turn into ghosts. This is a strange situation—the man is dying to leave the world, but his spirit wants to stay back. But if the number of ghosts goes up, it will be a huge problem. Earlier, ghosts used to dwell in the forests or in bamboo bushes outside the village or on banyan trees or inside abandoned houses. But now, such places are on the decline. So the ghosts are taking shelter in human hearts and changing their behaviour. Cases of people who look like human beings, but are actually ghosts are increasing day by day. Hence, yamdoots are instructed to be extra cautious in cases of suicides and accidents, where spirits must be dragged to the Mrityuloka as soon as they die.

The good thing in this case is that this girl would commit suicide in the morning. Statistics say that people mostly commit suicide at night. Why this happens is still a myth and needs serious research. In fact, studies are underway at many universities on the subject. Researchers have come to some kind of conclusion. One of the hypotheses says that people do not want to end their lives in the beginning of the day. End of any kind is dark and darkness cannot stand light. Others say waking up early in the morning is a bigger challenge than committing suicide! It could also be that the darkness of the night encourages them in their dark act. Plus, you can also escape the attention of others. Basically, no one wants to be seen committing suicide.

So, this case was going to be relatively easier—as the suicide was happening in the morning. According to earth time, it takes 45 minutes to reach Chitragupta's office from the world. And another 15 minutes for the official work.

But now it is almost eight o'clock and neither is any train visible nor any girl. At least be punctual while committing suicide!

Habul asked Babul, 'What's the name of the girl?'

'Which girl?'

'The one who'll commit suicide, who else?'

Babul took out a computer printout from the pocket and said, 'Sumati Samanta.'

Yamdoots are handed over computer printouts by Chitragupta. Details of the ones who will be dying are mentioned there: the name, address, age, a photograph and every other detail to ensure there is no difficulty in identifying the person. There is a reason behind introducing such a system. Once a middle-aged woman's spirit was to be brought to the Mrityuloka. She had so much make-up on, that by mistake the yamdoot ended up bringing her daughter's spirit instead. When this mistake was discovered after consulting the records, it was a source of huge embarrassment. All sorts of problems followed. The girl's spirit had to be restored and her mother's spirit had to be brought—double work! After a couple of such errors, this system was introduced.

'What does the word *Sumati* mean?' Habul asked.

'It means good thoughts or good intentions or simply a person with ample sense. *Su* means good. But she is actually a *Kumati*.'

'Now what does that mean?'

'*Ku* means bad. Does anyone with a '*su-mati*' commit suicide? It needs so much good karma to be born a human being. After so many births is one born a human being, and wasting that priceless life this way...'

'What's that to us? We are yamdoots. Our work is to fetch the souls of the dead, we are not supposed to think about anything else.'

'That is okay, but still... Why waste a life? How old would she be?'

'Twenty-two.'

'Tchach! Can anyone kill herself at such an age?'

'What is the issue with the age?'

'This is the age of vitality and of prime youth. At this age, people fight, they enjoy, they live.'

'How can there be an age for fighting? A fighter can fight at any age. It's all in the mind.'

'Brother Habul! Stop these sermons early in the morning. Let's find the girl.'

'Where do I look for her?'

'Look out! Is that the girl—slim girl with flowing hair, clad in a pink salwar-kameez hurrying towards us?'

Habul swiftly went off and returned at the speed of light.

'Yes, it is her. Oh! Such a young girl! Such a tender age!'

'Why are you sounding so emotional today, Habul? What's wrong?'

'I am missing my daughter, suddenly. She would be of the same age now. When I died she was doing her BA. I had gone to see her once, she was working with a private company.'

'Okay, okay! Now forget the past. What's done cannot be undone.'

'It's not that simple.'

'If you keep remembering the past, you will never forget it even after you are born again.'

'I don't mind that!'

'Life would become very difficult that way. You will never be committed to your life as a yamdoot, and will keep remembering your past. Take my word, forget your past. Let your past relations be.'

'Probably you are right.'

'The girl has come. Now we have to wait for the train. Our job would be done for the day but the train was scheduled at 7.13 a.m. Find out what's going to happen, do.'

Habul went off again and returned in some time with the news that in the last station there was a *rail-roko*. 'It will take some more time for the train to arrive.'

'Why, what has happened?'

'Inflation, rising prices... People are agitating. This is one of the modern ways of agitation: block the rail, block the road.'

'What is the relation between rising prices and the railways? Would stopping the train prevent price rise?'

'How can I say what will happen?'

'All that creates problems for the mortals all right, but now these 'rokos' are affecting us! Even Chitragupta cannot get the timing right while all this is going on. What can we do now?'

'Wait. That's the only thing you can do. Wait till the train arrives and this girl commits suicide.'

two

Sumati

On reaching the level crossing, Sumati looked at her watch. It is going to be 8 in the morning. After 7, a passenger train passes through this route. Sumati had thought she would commit suicide by jumping under the wheels of that train. If she was late, and the passenger train had left, then even a goods train would do.

There can be many ways of committing suicide—by hanging or poisoning or even cutting the wrist veins. However, Sumati desired to commit suicide by coming under a running train. She was trying to imagine what it would be like to commit suicide—the engine rushing towards her and she spreading herself on the tracks, just like a dead man is laid on the pyre. Following that, the train would cut her into pieces. The tracks would be smeared in blood. The stones, the rail and even the grass would be bloodstained. After a while, she would cease to exist. Is it too painful to go through the process? But she was afraid to come out in the night all alone—the road is lonely; the trees around might just have some ghosts. Especially, the huge gulmohar tree at the level crossing alone has about five ghosts. It is believed that all those who commit suicide here turn into evil spirits and ghosts. Usually ghosts prefer the peepul or bael (stone apple) trees. But there are no such trees at the level crossing; maybe that is why the ghosts have had to take shelter in the gulmohar tree. Would she become a ghost and frighten people from one of these trees? What would she look like after becoming a ghost? Would she have whiskers or tusks or huge ears like elephants? Or would she don long white hair and be adorned in a white saree, like they show in horror movies?

Following such thoughts about her possible future after the suicide, Sumati returned to the present. She has come out of her house with an objective which needs to be fulfilled. She has even left a suicide note—what if her father finds it and comes over to take her? But that won't be possible. He would still be hung-over. It will be around ten o'clock by the time he wakes up. But what if her younger brother saw the letter... Nah! Even he had not returned last night, which meant he won't be back before noon. He must be lying drunk in some club or at some friend's place. Mother committed suicide because her husband was alcoholic. After mom's death, her brother turned alcoholic having associated himself with all the wrong people.

What a life! The father an alcoholic, the brother an alcoholic...

And what about herself? What had she not done to become a film actress? But was it her doing completely? Was she responsible for the turn her life had taken?

She never thought her life would bring her to the railway tracks in this fashion. Being from a lower middle-class family, she had few possessions. Among what she had was beauty and very high aspirations. She was a resident of Bharatpur, located close to Bhubaneswar. When a city expands, its outskirts are slowly incorporated into it. When such a thing happens, the villages don't become cities; they do not remain villages either. They hang somewhere in between, and are often the worst places to live in. There is a sea change in the economy, culture and tradition of the village. And amidst this tornado of change, many fail to hold their ground, and with that, come to lose their moorings, their authenticity as individuals. One such man is Sumati's father, Loknath Samanta.

With the expansion of Bhubaneswar, the price of land

at Bharatpur started increasing. With the hopes of earning a lot of money as a land dealer, Loknath left his small grocery business. It worked wonders initially. Under such circumstances, it is tough to keep money earned suddenly, especially if the earner isn't used to it. It is tougher to resist oneself from indulging in vices. With money, came associating with the wrong kind of people. Even before money could come in properly, the ways to spend them became clear.

Sumati was nineteen or twenty then, a student of a college in the village. She was beautiful; yet she did not have the softness of a candle, but the fieriness of a forest fire. She aspired to act in movies. She dreamt of becoming a successful heroine. She imagined an entire Odisha going crazy for her. Like whenever she left home, there would be a traffic jam. She wanted to be a perfect heart-throb for the people. To realize her dreams, she became impatient to join the movie world. She worked with some amateur groups and also in some college plays. But that did not satisfy her. She wanted to be on the silver screen.

At this point, Butu Pati entered the scene. He wanted land in Bharatpur and got in touch with Loknath. There, Butu came to know of Sumati's desire. He told her that he knew several producers and getting her what she wants would hardly be a big deal for him. She already looked so beautiful, and she could act—she would certainly be a heroine.

Sumati thought that finally, fortune had begun to smile upon her. Even Loknath agreed: 'If the daughter earns money, what is the problem?' If anyone had a problem, it was Sumati's mother. But why should anyone listen to someone objecting to a source of income? A hefty one at that, possibly.

This was the time she met Subrata. He had fallen for her after seeing her act in the college plays. This could be called an ideal instance of love at first sight. Without the slightest hesitation, he professed his love for her. Even Sumati liked Subrata, but it's just that she did not want a relationship at that point. She did not want anything to hold her back—she just wanted to realize her dreams.

She clearly remembered that day. It was evening; a star or two lit the horizon. They disappeared only to return. They blinked. She had told Subrata, 'I cannot afford to be bound by your love. See that star, that is where I want to be.' Subrata had replied, 'The path that you have chosen for yourself is obscure. Be sure of what you want.' Sumati had replied, 'I never looked ahead to be pulled back.' Tears had gathered in Subrata's eyes, but he had suppressed the excruciating pain he was experiencing and only wished her all the best. 'But do remember that I love you and always will,' was what he said before leaving. He did not return for the next few years.

And so much happened during that time. Butu Pati took her to the producer of a music album.

'But I want to be a film heroine, not a face in a music album,' Sumati said.

Butu Pati said, 'You will rise step by step. First you have to read in classes I and II before your graduation. First perform the dance item in the album.'

She performed—she danced as she was told.

She saw herself on the television screen, but she was not happy. In the days that followed, Sumati's world turned upside down.

On the one hand, Butu Pati's repeated assurances... Just a few more days... And on the other, Loknath's worsening drinking habit. In no time, he had made a nosedive into an abysmal pit of decline, all for more money. More money...

Sumati's mother's efforts of trying to set things right, failed. Even Sumati's brother began being in the wrong company. Unrest at home increased. Failing to tolerate what was happening around her, Sumati's mother, a woman of modest ambition, committed suicide. After this, Loknath's recklessness increased—Sumati was forced to act in amateur plays to earn fast cash. She did get some roles in television, but very small ones, with small production houses. The dream of becoming the number one Odia actress became bleaker and bleaker.

At this point, Butu Pati informed Sumati that a director wants her as actress. She was asked to come for a screen test in the evening. She felt uneasy about the situation. Her father told her to go and she went. Sumati was offered a cup of tea. She fell unconscious and each time she felt she was coming back to her senses, she could sense being covered with worms, snakes and hyenas. The next morning when she woke up, she found herself in a stranger's bed, completely naked and with a lot of pain all over her body—a pain surpassed only by mental agony.

She knew what had happened to her.

Somehow she managed to return home. She informed her father that she would not go to that place anymore.

'Why not? You would earn money!'

'They are not good people. You don't know what they have done to me.'

'How does it matter? You will be getting money.'

'To what extent can I compromise for money, Baba?'

'For money you can do anything. You better do.'

'No, I cannot do this. Not anymore.'

'Of course you have to go! I have already taken money in advance.'

If a father wants such a life for her daughter, what is the point in living? The only way to escape the situation is dying. It is true that she wanted to be a film actress, but not like this, not by subjecting herself to the gnawing of the hyenas, the bites of the snakes and scorpions. She remembered Subrata; she had refused him for her career and this is what her dreams had brought her to. She had told him that she wanted nothing to hold her back. She had pointed to the star and said that she wanted to reach as far as that. Today, she is actually on her way to leave the world.

Good human beings become stars. But is she one? She remembered everything that happened to her that night and that feeling of being dragged through mud and slush with snakes and scorpions.

The train is getting late but she could just about see smoke, now she could see the train coming. Here is the sound... Goodbye, Mother Earth!

three

Subrata

The level crossing gate at Bharatpur is closed. Subrata turned off the ignition of the motorbike. Why waste petrol? He took out his handkerchief and wiped the sweat on his forehead. It is still not eight in the morning and look at the heat! He turned back and checked if his bag on the motorcycle is all right. Inside the bag, there are samples of several medicines.

Subrata is a medical representative. He was a student of science. He had once dreamt of becoming a well-known doctor, but that never happened. Subrata had many dreams since childhood, but somehow nothing could materialize. He likes literature, poetry. He had also contemplated studying literature, but his father was opposed to the idea. To go with his father's wishes, he took up science. While studying science, he dreamt of being a doctor. He took the entrance test to study medicine, but could not clear it. After failing at the very first step, he realized that he could never be a doctor. So what would he do? After graduating with biology, he went for an MBA. This time too, his father decided what he should study. He thought that he would work in some reputed company as a manager, but that did not happen either.

Honestly, there was no chance. Subrata could never concentrate on his studies. Ever since Sumati left, he was psychologically shattered. But he never blamed Sumati. The kind of family Subrata is from, a job is the only thing he would do after completing his education; there was no chance of him trying his luck in business or any other profession that did not guarantee a good future. Moreover, he did not have the money or the guts required to start a business. After appearing for several job interviews, at last Subrata became a medical representative.

What is his job? To carry a bag and go from one doctor to another, to wait outside their chambers—sometimes sit and sometimes stand beneath the lamp post. If the doctors give him a chance, he will get to talk about the medicines of his company. On most occasions, they would not even listen to him. Then he would give them sample medicines and request them to prescribe those medicines to patients. He would also be carrying small gifts—a pen, writing pad, etc. But these days, the medicine companies are not giving small gifts anymore. They are giving more expensive gifts to doctors to lure them, so that the chances of them recommending their product go up. Some companies are inviting the doctors and their families to conferences at five-star hotels. At times, such conferences are being organized abroad—this way the entire job is completed at one go. They would get to attend the conference and also get a chance to go to a foreign country. Initially, however, Subrata did not like the job. But after three years in this profession, it has become a part of his life. One becomes immune after a point. Subrata has.

He kept his handkerchief inside his pocket and looked around. There are not too many people. At the corner of the road, a young lady in a pink salwar-kameez is looking towards the train. The face of the girl looks familiar... Her expressions are known. The girl looked at her watch and Subrata got a shock—it felt as if an electric current passed through his body.

Oh my God! This is Sumati!

My God! After so many years!

His heart skipped beats. Within moments, a thousand memories crowded his mind.

Subrata parked his motorcycle at the side of the road and rushed towards Sumati. What is she doing on the railway tracks? The train is approaching.

The train was almost there, and suddenly Subrata realized that Sumati was rushing towards it. He reacted instantly. With his heart in his mouth, he ran with vigour and speed. People at the level crossing looked on, stunned.

Somehow, he pulled Sumati back in the split second that separated her body and the train. Both fell on the stones along the track as the train whistled past. A shocking pain rocketed throughout their bodies. The sound of the train reverberated through their spines—just a feet, or maybe a little less than that! Subrata had never felt death in such proximity.

After the train went past, many people gathered at the place. Sumati fell unconscious. She had hurt herself badly. Both of them were bleeding profusely. Somehow Subrata got up and managed to bring Sumati back to the level crossing. Subrata defied his pain and requested the people who had gathered at the spot, 'Please park my motorcycle, somewhere. I have to take her to the hospital.'

The next couple of hours saw one incident tumbling over the other. Subrata had not seen as many facets of human beings in the past twenty-nine years of his life as he did on that day. He saw people who were completely unsympathetic. He saw people who wanted to make money out of the helplessness that others felt... 'It looks like an accident case, go report to the police', was what most of them at the hospital said.

'I do not have the time, doctor.'

'So what can we do? Unless there is a police report, we cannot treat her.'

Subrata burst his lungs out, 'First admit her. I'll burn the whole damn hospital down if something happens to her.'

Hearing the scream, some doctors and nurses stepped ahead. He happened to know one of the doctors who eventually decided to treat Sumati. 'If you had delayed by even a second, it might have been fatal. But she is still not out of danger. She has bled profusely. She is also suffering from intense shock and trauma. Let's see what can be done... Sister, please take her to the ICU. Quick!'

four

Incidents, One after Another

The sound of the train could still be heard. It kept echoing.

Sumati opened her eyes. The white ceiling appeared clearly after a strange haze that had blurred her vision. Slowly, the picture cleared. She could see a fan revolving—maybe it was white at one point. But it had turned grey with years of dust on it, just like her soul. The fan was revolving slowly and making a noise. *Khat khat khat khat...* Sumati looked around. There is a tube light—on-off, on-off. There was a sound *pring qurr pring*. On—light; off—darkness: a strange war ensued between light and darkness.

But how did she come here? Where is she? She was on the tracks. The train was there. Has she survived? How could she have done that? The last thing she remembers is her jumping before the train. But just before the head struck the tracks, there was a pull. That is all. Who pulled her back from death?

She looked to the other side. Two anxious eyes were looking down at her.

Subrata!

Subrata!

Subrata, whom she had left; to whom she had said that she wanted to move ahead and rise and rise in life. The same Subrata who would have been an impediment to her!

Subrata, here? Does that mean it was he who had saved her life? Sumati looked into the eyes of Subrata and discovered the sea of love. A time comes in life when you know the truth in a split second. It was that defining moment. Sumati came to realize the depth of Subrata's love for her today.

And at that moment she thought she needed to tell everything that had happened to her to Subrata. Now. So Sumati narrated to Subrata the dark story of her life. While being amidst the ocean between consciousness and subconsciousness, she kept muttering all that had happened with her in the last couple of years. Sumati thought it was necessary now to tell everything to Subrata, although she was hardly conscious. Everything about her dreams and them falling apart. Everything that had happened with her, Subrata should know... At that instant, Subrata said, 'You don't have to talk now, I'll listen to everything, every word that you say. But not now.'

Sumati said, 'No! I need to tell everything, everything. Now!' She sobbed as she spoke. She murmured. She stuttered. But she didn't stop until she fell unconscious. She started again after regaining consciousness. Soon it was all silent and dark...again.

five

Yamraj's Problem

Yamraj 5003 realized he was in deep trouble. Sumati was supposed to have committed suicide under a train, but Subrata has saved her at the last moment and has now taken her to the hospital. Yamraj went to the hospital. Yamraj 5003 knows not only this one but all the hospitals in Odisha. He has been to so many of them so many times. He even knows the doctors so well that he can predict whose patient will go to Yamloka early.

In government-run hospitals, patients die early and that's not without reason. Most government hospitals don't have sufficient facilities—it takes two hours to find a simple oxygen cylinder! Even after getting it, there is no guarantee that it will have oxygen. Then again, many patients are brought to these hospitals at the very last stage. At many nursing homes, when they realize that the final moments of the patient have arrived, they ask them to be taken to the government hospitals. 'Let them die there so that they don't create any commotion here', is the attitude.

But this time, it was very strange. Doctors of the government hospital to which Sumati had been taken, battled hard. Sumati was saved, despite all odds. If Yamraj wanted, however, he could have taken Sumati's life when she was in the ICU. But looking at Subrata's face and realizing how much he loved her, Yamraj somehow could not do so. When Subrata was praying with all his might for Sumati's life, had Yamraj taken her life, he would surely have lost all faith in God. It was, after all, such a young life.

Now Sumati has been shifted to a room. Much time has already been wasted. Sumati's spirit has to be taken to Mrityuloka, but Yamraj's heart is somehow holding him back. The love that Subrata had and the way he bound her by that, melted Yamraj 5003's heart. He could not imagine taking her away. The poet's cells in his brain were at work.

But duty is duty—he has to do it at any cost. Yamraj went to Sumati's room with his mace. The yamdoots followed. Their work won't be over until the girl dies. Babul let out a deep breath. 'Oh! Today, Yamloka had Rambha's dance programme,' he sighed. He loves Rambha's dance.

These days, many heroines are arriving at the Yamloka; they are even entertaining the inhabitants of Yamloka with their dance performances from time to time. Dance, as in some music and the movement of various parts of the body on the beats. In Hindi films, they call it an item number. Babul's ears turn red while watching these dance items. Worldly desires invade his mind. But he does not enjoy such dance programmes for long. Rambha's dance, however, he could watch for ages. But now all that seems to be going for a toss. How can he leave now? He can only leave after taking Sumati's soul. If he would have come with any other Yamraj, the job would have been over by now. This Yamraj Number 5003 is different. He gets emotional every time he comes to take a young person's soul. This time it seems he has become more emotional. What could be done!

Babul and Habul waited eagerly as Yamraj went into the room. Now, probably he will get the spirit of the girl.

As they waited, Babul's handheld communication device—something like the ubiquitous mobile phone—rang. When yamdoots come to the earth, they are given a device that even shows the caller's picture. It was Chitragupta's call. Babul doesn't like Chitragupta at all! He is very abusive. If he takes the call now, he will get an earful for being delayed. He will have to give all sorts of explanations. Disgusting! He switched off the device. If explanations have to be given, he will but all that once. Why do it again and again?

six

The Subrata-Yamraj Conversation

Subrata had fallen asleep on a chair beside Sumati's bed. Apart from the emotional turmoil in the past twelve odd hours, there had been tremendous strain and anxiety. At 11 in the night, the doctors told Subrata that Sumati was out of danger and the crisis had somehow been avoided. Subrata kept looking at Sumati, her scattered hair, so sick and so sad. His heart almost burst in pain. He said to himself that he will never let her go away from him. Never.

It was night, and a sudden feeling of cold draughts blowing past the room woke Subrata up. He had switched off the light. There was a faint ray of light through the curtains and it spread itself just like a drop of ink does on a blotting paper. In the interstice formed from the interplay of light and darkness, Subrata saw a huge figure standing in front of him. He wore a king-like crown, held a mace and had armlets.

Subrata was amazed! At this hour, such a man in a city hospital? An eerie sensation passed through his spine. Suddenly, he felt that he had seen an image resembling the figure somewhere. Thunder struck outside and Subrata suddenly realized he was Yamraj. Is this him? At this hour?

Not being able to comprehend what he should do, Subrata said, 'Pranam Yamraj.'

Yamraj 5003 was taken aback. This is not what he had expected. A living man cannot generally see him, how could this youth? Yamraj suddenly remembered that someone very close to the dying could, in fact, see him for a second. Even then, it is a rare thing, especially in today's world, where no one is close to anybody.

'Blessings, my son.'

'But why are you here?'

'I have come to take Sumati's soul. It is time for her to leave the world.'

'Sumati's soul?'

'Yes, son!'

'But I just got her and you are here to take her away once again?'

'Who am I? Who will come to the earth and who will

leave it behind is decided by the Almighty, my son. My work is just to take the soul when it is time.'

'But…but I won't let her go.'

'Why?'

'I love her.'

'Love? Someone who left you?'

'Left me! When? Lord, I have a poem for you.'

'Poem?'

'Yes.

> *The stars ask me,*
> *Do you still expect her back?*
> *My smiling heart says,*
> *Never believed that she left.'*

'What does that mean? Say it simply.'

'I reside in Sumati, my Lord. How can you take her away?'

'You reside in her? What do you mean?'

'Surely you have been to Chilika?'

'Chilika? That lake?'

'Yes!'

'I have been there. So?'

'Every year during winter, migratory birds arrive there. After winter, all of them go back.'

'So? What is the connection?'

'The love of some people is like these birds—they keep coming and going. And the love of some birds is like the lotus of the village pond. When water dries up, the lotus vanishes. The moment the pond returns, the lotus does too. My love is like the lotus. It may not always be visible but it can never altogether be lost. I dwell in her heart. Always did. Where could she have gone?'

'Is it? Such deep love? But had she not left you and moved on?'

'Have you ever closed your fist and tried to hold the water as it falls? You have to spread your palms out and bend it a little to create a space to help it stay within. Love is like that water that you cannot hold with your palms closed. Love, my Lord, is no shackle. Freedom is the essence of love. You don't expect anything in return for true love. I have always loved her truly and that is why I never wanted to hold her back. I always believed if my love was strong, she would come back some day.'

'I understand that my child. But her time is over. Let her go.'

'Where is her fault, tell me, my Lord. Why should she commit suicide? The ones who drove her to this state, the ones who raped her and ruined her life, they are spared and she has to die? Is this what you call justice, *Prabhu?*'

'You can't judge God's sense of justice in individual cases. You have to see it in a larger perspective.'

'Maybe, but for me, I cannot see any of it. My Lord, all that we see is gross violation of justice.'

'The system of justice has various levels. It is not so easy to understand. Let me do my job.'

'I won't, I can't. If you have to take her, you have to take my life too.'

'Your time in this world is not over yet.'

'If you take her, I would be left with no reason to live. I will be a dead man walking. What use is such life?'

'Don't say that. Someone's death cannot hinder another. Life moves on, you would too. After Sumati leaves today, you will be sad for a few days; after that you will also move on. She had left you. Did you anticipate this would happen? Did you ever think that you would get her back this way?'

'Sumati is in my blood, my heart, my veins. She may not have been there with me in person, but she was always there with me, in my heart. And now that I have got her again... No... If she is gone, I shall have to go too. She is in my soul. No, my Lord! If you take her, you got to take me too. We are now one. Don't separate us.'

'That is not possible, my child! There is a law of nature that has to be followed.'

Yamraj threw his rope over Sumati. He started getting ready to take the spirit of the girl. Subrata realized she was slipping away. He knelt at Yamraj's feet. Yamraj started getting angry.

'Let me do my work. Don't let me use force.'

Subrata's world was tearing to pieces. He has always been dictated and directed by others. This is probably the first time in his life that he found his voice. His back was right against the wall.

'Do all that you can, my Lord. But I won't let you take her.'

'I know you love her a lot. More than your life. But there's no way that I can go back without taking her.'

'Why can you not, my Lord? Just think, when did she live a life? She just tried to live life her way. She was deceived, but she always had the desire to live. Please give her one last chance. Give us the opportunity to live together…please!'

Yamraj saw that a young man was begging for the life of a girl who had once deserted him. For a girl who had once said that to move ahead in life, you cannot have anyone holding you back. The young man was ready to give up his life for this girl. Yamraj started thinking. Again. The ice began to melt. It was as if a flower blossomed on a piece of stone.

Habul and Babul saw Yamraj removing the rope from Sumati. They saw Yamraj hugging Subrata while telling him that there is an end to all ends. 'From one end starts the beginning of another. So get a new life. Start life afresh. Every beginning has an end and every end a beginning. Just when it seemed everything was over, you start living, now.'

Ever since Habul and Babul became yamdoots, they had never seen anything like this. This is the first time since the Savitri-Satyavan incident, in which Savitri, daughter of Madra kingdom's Asvapati saved the life of her husband Satyavan from Yamraj—that a dead person, or someone who was destined to die, was being granted life. They looked at Yamraj and were dumbfounded.

Yamraj said, 'Let's go. Let's go back to Mrityuloka. Would you keep sitting here or what?'

Habul said, 'If we don't take the soul, Chritragupta will be angry.'

Yamraj said, 'We shall see what happens. I have given Sumati's life back. Can't take it back now.'

seven

Chitragupta's Problem

Chitragupta was sitting in his office. This is where Yamraj brings the soul of the dead after which the accounts of the person's deeds during his or her lifetime are adjudged and then punishment decided. It was around 11 a.m. At this time of the day, the office is relatively empty. The souls usually come at night. Therefore, Chitragupta can breathe slightly easy between 7 in the morning and 1 in the afternoon. Go to a hospital and the reason behind this would be clear. All the people become occupied in the mornings. Children go to schools, elders go to their respective workplaces, old men go to libraries or simply nod off, housewives—after doing their cooking—become busy with domestic chores, the ones who watch television are struck by drowsiness; and if you happen to switch off the television, assuming they are asleep, they will spring right up and charge you, 'Why did you switch the TV off?' Mornings and early noon time are therefore not appropriate times for death. Night-time is best for people to leave the world. A sheet of darkness envelopes the world and nothing but silence is audible. Like a spider stuck in its web moving towards insects, its prey, night-time has a quality that is mysterious. Daytime does not do justice to death. It takes darkness to create the mystique surrounding death.

Until some four or five years ago, the situation was thus. After the nerve-racking work at night, Chitragupta and his officials could just relax for a while. But with this population explosion over the past decade, there is nothing like a 'fixed time'. People have now started dying at any time. Most of the road and rail accidents happen in early mornings, as the drivers tend to doze off.

The other day, a yamdoot working in Chitragupta's office at Mrityuloka made an interesting remark: 'Look at the world; no cold in winter; there is drought and suddenly there is flood; high pressure and again there is a low pressure. This world is going to the dogs—no certainty with the climatic changes, not even a fixed time for death.'

Earlier, the time of someone's death used to be predestined by God. That too is gradually changing. In fact, maybe human beings are tampering with their destiny.

The one who has suffered the most as a result of all this commotion is Chitragupta. He has already decided that he will have to bring this issue up to the Trinity—Brahma, Vishnu and Maheshwar. Let them take some difficult decisions.

Today, Chitragupta's office is relatively empty. In a relaxed manner he was going through a business magazine. He loves business magazines—it suggests the various ways in which the worldly mortals are striving to become richer and richer, and quickly. Whether anyone becomes rich after reading all this is a separate issue. In the Mrityuloka, however, the concepts of being poor and rich are non-existent. If anyone has something more than he needs, he is rich, and if someone has less than what he needs, he is poor. In the land of the dead, no one has anything. Therefore, there is no class division here. But despite all this, Chitragupta loves the magazine. The idea that someone can be rich without putting in hard work amuses him a great deal. Such magazines are not printed in the Mrityuloka though. There is no newspaper or magazine here. The sole journalist, Narad, disseminates news in the archaic way in all the three *lokas*. His ways are simple: he tells someone something that someone else, in turn, says to someone else and so on. But the problem with information passing from person to person is that news gets distorted. That is why no one believes in the news spread in Mrityuloka. There, it's all rumours.

The magazine that Chitragupta is reading has arrived from the world last night itself. A sharebroker died; he was reading this very magazine in his last few minutes, when he suffered a massive heart attack. He was reading the reasons behind the sudden crash of shares of a company at the time. Yamraj rushed to take his spirit, but the way it clung on to the magazine he had to exert a lot of pressure to take it away. Such cases are becoming more and more common. The other day someone died of a heart attack since the cricket team he supported lost. Following his death, he got stuck to the television screen on which the match was being broadcast. After trying every possible way, Yamraj had to bring the entire television set along with the spirit, of course. Now the man watches cricket matches in heaven. You might be thinking how he could manage to go to heaven. Simple. He never left his house and always watched cricket. Since he never went out, he never became jealous, misbehaved or harmed anyone. He never committed any sin. Therefore, he had no reason to be in hell. It is like someone who stays drunk and does no wrong in his life. He goes to heaven and maintains his earthly habits. In the world he drinks earthly wine, and in heaven, he drinks *somras*.

At this time, a yamdoot informed him that Yamraj 1987 is coming with two spirits. Chitragupta kept his magazine aside and returned to work. He switched the computer on. He got the machine a couple of years back and has been using it ever since. Initially, he had difficulty adjusting with the machine, but now he is used to it. In fact, he understands working on a computer is far easier than doing everything manually. It saves him a lot of time and labour. At times he wonders how he could ever manage without a computer.

The two spirits arrived following Yamraj 1987. He told Chitragupta, 'Assess their deeds and report to the main Yamraj for him to take a decision about their reward or punishment. I am tired...going to rest for a while.'

The two people who came began arguing. Chitragupta saw these men were Odias who had died in a road accident. One of them was a preacher, the other, the driver of the auto that had met with an accident—both were from Bhubaneswar. The preacher was in his saffron robe, had long hair, a rudraksh around his neck, rings containing a variety of stones on his fingers and also a golden chain. The auto driver was also in his apparel. Worn-out jeans, and a red vest which had 'tata' and 'bye bye' written on its front and back. He also wore bangles and sacred threads he had gathered from different temples of Bhubaneswar. He did not want to disappoint any of the Gods. Wherever there is an auto stand in Bhubaneswar, there is a temple and at each temple these threads are sold. He had threads from all the temples. Like the traffic police, even the Gods are to be kept happy. His girlfriend had said affectionately that with that steel bangle, he looked like a goonda. To be an auto driver in Bhubaneswar you got to look like one, though. Without religion and some muscle power, living in the city has become a difficult job.

Chitragupta asked them to wait, as the judgement from the Yamraj would take some time to arrive and only after that would it be decided where they were to go.

The preacher asked, 'Meaning?'

'Yamraj will decide your fate. If you are to go to hell, which of the twenty-one hells. And if you are to go to heaven there are different types—deluxe and ordinary. Your deeds will be factored in before you are sent to the right place.'

The auto driver and preacher went into the waiting room. Chitragupta sent their reports to Yamraj. After some time, a Yamdoot brought a piece of paper from inside and handed it over to Chitragupta. Chitragupta called both the preacher and the auto driver to announce Yamraj's verdict.

'What happened?' both of them asked.

'Mr Preacher, you shall go to heaven. An ordinary room has been allotted to you.'

'Sir, what about me?' the auto driver asked, nervously.

'You will also go to heaven. A deluxe room has been allotted to you.'

Now the preacher became very angry and was in a state of shock. It is an established fact that man feels worse when someone else is in a better position, be it in life or death. It is not in human nature to stand the good of another.

The preacher said, 'This is sheer injustice! Through my sermons, I show people the ways of religion; even those who moved away from it are brought back. I shall stay in an ordinary room and the auto driver will stay in a deluxe room? This, despite you knowing that his driving style brought me here?'

The preacher's high-pitched voice attracted the main Yamraj's attention. He came out and addressed the priest's grievance. Yamraj was calm in his reply.

'You want to know why you have been allotted an ordinary room and the auto driver a deluxe room?'

'Yes! I deserve to know, tell me. Everyone knows there is a difference between my work and his. It is like heaven and hell. And yet this judgement!'

'When you give your sermons, half the people sleep.

When he drives his auto, everyone in it remembers God and prays for their safety. More people have remembered the Almighty in his auto than they have after hearing your sermons. Tell me, whose work is nobler? Remember, your work is important, not your position. At least in the Mrityuloka, it is performance, not position that counts.

The preacher stood silent. He was in a state of shock and utter disbelief.

'Take them to their respective rooms in heaven,' Yamraj ordered.

Two yamdoots came and took them away.

Yamraj asked Chitragupta, 'Is anyone else scheduled to come?'

Chitragupta looked into his computer and said, 'Yamraj 5003 was supposed to bring a young girl's spirit who was to die at 7 a.m. But he has not returned yet. It is already about an hour late.' Chitragupta thought, Yamraj would express his concern, but none of that happened.

'Okay, Shyamala has called, I am going home. Process the file of this girl and keep me posted.'

Having said this, Yamraj left on his buffalo.

Chitragupta looked on after Yamraj left. Shyamala is Yamraj's wife. So the Yamraj goes home when his wife wants him to, but Chitragupta cannot leave office. He wants to go home but since Yamraj is gone, he cannot and despite being tired he has to stay on. It felt as if someone pricked his heart with a thorn. After all, he is also Brahma's son, but look at him! He is having to work as Yamraj's subordinate, a clerk. He is the one keeping track of all living beings, and everyone remembers only Yamraj. His work goes unrecognized.

He let out a deep breath. He remembered his past. Yamraj was given the responsibility of Mrityuloka. He was told that he is supposed to keep an account of everyone and deliver them justice after their death. Yamraj said, 'I will deliver justice all right, but is it possible for me to do all the work alone?'

He went and told Brahma about the problem. Brahma started his meditation that went on for 11,000 years. Then, when he opened his eyes, Brahma saw a man shrouded with tranquillity, with a pen and an inkpot, and a shawl tied to his waist. Brahma said to him, 'You are born from my *manaspat* in a *gupt* manner, in secrecy. Therefore, you shall be named Chitragupta. You will award the ones who will be religious and righteous, and punish the wrongdoers. Having originated from my *kaya*, your progenies would be called Kayastha.'

Chitragupta is not an ordinary being. In the scriptures, it is said he initiated the script. In the Puranas, it is written that before a ritual, one has to remember and offer him prayers. Even after a man dies, Chitragupta is to be remembered during the last few minutes of his life.

But despite everything, what is his status? A clerk at Mrityuloka—an accountant of sorts. Yamraj can tell him, 'I am going home, you send me the details', but can he say the same thing to Yamraj? A rage was simmering inside of him. He started burning from within.

He looked at the computer screen. Yamraj 5003 was supposed to take out the soul of the girl at 7.13 a.m. and then it should have taken him another one hour to reach here. They should have been at his office latest by nine. Chitragupta had thought that after Yamraj 5003 reached office with the soul of the girl, he would go home. But it is well past nine. Why is Yamraj 5003 still not coming? There could be a traffic jam. But no way should they have been so late.

Chitragupta has enough reasons to be annoyed with Yamraj 5003. He is kind of strange, not serious with anything, cannot do his work at the right time, he is always distracted with something or the other. What he thinks, what he does—only he knows. No one knows what Prajapita Brahma did while making Yamraj 5003 and Chitragupta has to suffer for it now.

He went back to his magazine. Money is a strange commodity—tough with it and tougher without. But the point is that there is no one in the world who does not want money. Money is like a beautiful girl—look at her and you feel good but after some time you feel jealous, because somebody else will have her. Thank God, money is useless here. However, whenever Chitragupta reads about money, he feels good. But today even this magazine could not relieve him. After a six- or seven-year gap, it seems recession is returning to the world. In India, inflation has shot up. The Indian economy could again be hit by a downturn. This made him even sadder. There is no direct relation between Chitragupta and the Indian economy but still he feels unhappy when there is a report of any downturn. He doesn't like it when people are sad.

When it was past noon, Chitragupta started getting tense. What is delaying Yamraj 5003 so much? He kept his magazine aside, switched on the computer and opened the file of the one whose soul was to be brought. It showed the details—Name: Sumati, Age: 22. Her past was documented briefly. Chitragupta read it carefully—hmm, interesting case. But in the end, the girl is committing suicide. Suicide is a sin, which means she is certainly going to go to hell. Chitragupta saw that Habul and Babul had accompanied

Yamraj 5003. Both of them are experienced yamdoots. He tried to contact them. There is a separate device, specially designed to communicate with the yamrajs and yamdoots. Yamraj 5003 did not respond to the call and Habul's device was not working. Babul's device did. Babul said, 'Maharaj, I am at the hospital.'

'Hospital? What are you doing there? You are supposed to bring the soul from Bharatpur railway crossing.'

'It is a long story. Can't talk much now. We are at the hospital and trying to leave as early as possible.'

Chitragupta heard an exasperated sigh. After that the phone was switched off. Nothing could be done till they returned with the soul. Chitragupta went to his home, but he was seriously worried. His wife had cooked good food but he could not enjoy the lunch. You can't enjoy anything when you are tense. He was most displeased with Yamraj 5003. He could not even enjoy Rambha's dance in the afternoon. The sun descended and it was night. Now Chitragupta was really ill at ease. There had still been no news about Yamraj 5003. Both Habul and Babul had switched off their devices. The night grew deeper. Not being able to go home, Chitragupta fell asleep. He did not know how long he had been sleeping. Suddenly, a yamdoot informed that Yamraj 5003 had crossed Baitarani. It was a matter of time before he reached.

Chitragupta saw that the eastern side of the horizon was turning red. It was almost dawn. He had spent the whole night in the same room—his body started aching. It is Mrityuloka all right; nobody suffers from any ailment here, but he is getting old. Yamraj 5003 is the culprit! Had he not been there, everything would have been in place, he thought.

Yamraj 5003 finally arrived with Habul and Babul in tow. Usually, the spirits have to be dragged with a rope and brought to hell. At times, even that does not work. The two ferocious two-headed dogs haul them along. Why such a small number of souls come to this land on their own is something Chitragupta could not understand. Everybody wants to go to heaven, but nobody is ready to die! Everyone knows that death is inevitable and yet they try their best to stop themselves from dying when the time comes. These mortals find the world particularly attractive. Despite experiencing so much pain, disease, dissatisfaction, most people want to live. Even after death, most of them want to go back to the world. Even if they cannot be born as a human, they still like to return as a bird or some animal. A poet wrote:

> *I'll return as a bird,*
> *And will make all the fields my own.*

Even the ones who die willingly, do not arrive at the Mrityuloka easily; they are always planning to continue staying in the world as ghosts. But wait, something is wrong.

Chitragupta asked, 'Where is Sumati's soul?'

Yamraj 5003 replied, 'Did not get it.'

'*Did not get it?* Did the spirit turn into a ghost and flee? You had two yamdoots, both experienced. What happened?'

'No. It has not turned into a ghost.'

'Then?'

'I have left the soul in the world.'

'*Left it!*'

'Yes. I granted Sumati a new life.'

'*What the hell do you mean?*'

'Yes. I gave her a new life. I let her go. That's all.'

The way Yamraj 5003 was speaking, Chitragupta became severely enraged. He said, 'How dare you do such a thing? This is against the norms of the Mrityuloka.'

'I am a Yamraj. This is Mrityuloka, my abode. I can do whatever I wish to.'

'You might be the Lord of Mrityuloka. But you don't have the right to break the rules.'

'Of course I can break a rule.'

'Says who? You don't have the right to do any such thing.'

'I don't know about right and wrong. I saw the love

between Sumati and Subrata and my heart melted. I gave Sumati a new life and came back here. I think it is fair. I shall speak no more.'

'Your heart melted? You are a Yamraj and you say your heart melted? You are *not* supposed to have a heart that melts! *Just go and get her soul.*'

After toiling for an entire day, followed by a sleepless night and then the long distance between the world and the Mrityuloka, Yamraj 5003 was completely exhausted. Already fatigued, Chitragupta's words infuriated him. He controlled himself somehow, and said: 'See Chitragupta, whatever I have done is my job. Your work is to keep a track of man's sins and his good work. Don't poke your nose into my affairs.'

This only added fuel to the fire.

Chitragupta shouted back, 'What do you think? You think you can do anything you want? There are certain norms, nobody is above rules.'

Yamraj 5003 was taken aback. Normally, Chitragupta is a calm person. What is wrong with him? His tone angered him further: 'Ordinary clerk, how dare you even speak against the Yamraj?'

Now Yamraj raised his voice further and said: 'Hold your tongue. Do you know who you are speaking to?'

'I know who you are. You, Yamraj 5003, are supposed to

bring the souls of the dead to me. This is about your work.'

The voices kept getting louder.

'Shut up you! Chitragupta! Just one knock from this mace and you'll retire for six months.'

'You are threatening me!'

'It is not just a threat. I shall do it, if you don't shut up right now. You want me to do it?'

He then raised his mace and surged ahead. Such heated argument between Chitragupta and a Yamraj is unprecedented. The yamdoots looked on, shocked and dumbstruck. Even they did not know what to do. Should they interfere? They could not understand how to react. They have already seen a lot of new things in the past day. Habul and Babul had never seen Yamraj 5003 in such a bad mood. But when Yamraj 5003 almost attacked Chitragupta, Habul rushed ahead and held his hand. By chance if he actually hit Chitragupta, it would cause utter tumult in the whole Triloka. Habul said, 'What are you doing, my Lord? What will you get by hitting this mosquito-like creature? Please calm down. You are exhausted. Please go and take some rest.'

Yamraj 5003 left the room led by Habul and Babul. But Chitragupta was hissing like a snake. His anger knew no bounds. 'How dare the Yamraj behave like this? I am

Brahma's son. I keep track of what is going on in the whole damn world! What does he think I am? I will not forget this insult. From today, I shall not do any work till this issue is resolved.'

eight

Commotion in Heaven

The news of the altercation and fight between Yamraj 5003 and Chitragupta spread rapidly. Such a thing had never happened in the history of Yamloka. A fight between Chitragupta and Yamraj! Old Gods and Goddesses said, 'Nosedive in values! See the condition of Mrityuloka! Such incidents happen only on earth! The threat of an assault in Mrityuloka? Fie for shame!' Some Gods expressed deep concern that the universe might not continue if there is a fight between Yamraj and Chitragupta.

Innumerable discussions followed over the cause of the dispute. Yamraj had gone to the world to bring the soul of a girl but returned empty-handed. This is a once-in-a-million-year phenomenon. Seeing the condition of Savitri, Satyavan was given a new lease of life. Vishnu and Maheshwar have also done this a couple of times in the distant past. But such a thing has happened after thousands of years. And Yamraj 5003 has done this!

♣

The moment Narad came to know of this, he became very happy. The news spread like black clouds during monsoon. It would be incorrect to say he was entirely 'happy'. Pleasure is a pure experience. Narad's pleasure was not, however, a pure one; there was anger juxtaposed with it and there was also a feeling of being vindicated. It was because of this Yamraj that Brahma had insulted him. Insult Narad! Insult a journalist! He had kept his feelings concealed in his heart for such a long time. Today, he has his opportunity. This is the time to take revenge against the one who was instrumental in having him insulted. A serpent inside Narad's heart awoke from hibernation and started crawling to the fore. Narad left for Vishnuloka. He took on his dhenki and reached Vishnuloka in a very short time.

Vishnu was resting, keeping his head on Lakshmi's lap. He was in a romantic mood. Narad went straight to his place. Seeing Narad, Lakshmi went inside. Vishnu got up. Both were a little embarrassed.

Narad ignored all this and came straight to the point.

'Prabhu, what is this?'

Vishnu asked, 'What? What happened?'

'What is this problem?'

'What problem? Why are you so disturbed about?'

Vishnu loves Narad, but he gets hyper often. That seems to be his main problem. He also has a second problem—he enters any place at any time and has little respect for others' privacy. But you cannot tell him anything—he is a journalist after all. Be it among the Gods or among men, journalists are revered beings and they merrily intrude into your private space. They have scant regard for others' privacy.

Narad said, 'Yamraj is appropriating your powers.'

'*Munivar*, you are talking in English way too much these days. The ways of the world appears to have affected you. But please don't talk in such difficult English in Vishnuloka.'

'Prabhu, you are thinking about these silly things? The world there is going to the dogs!'

'Which world?'

'The world that Brahma created so painstakingly and you are nurturing with so much care.'

'Why? What is wrong?'

'Yamraj has appropriated your powers. Putting it simply, Yamraj is taking over your powers.'

'What do you mean?'

'Yamraj has started granting lives to people.'

'Let him. Sparing lives is a very good thing. Everyone should do it.'

'You are not giving due importance to the incident. I am talking about a new life given to the dead. Only you used to do this.'

Narad deliberately did not mention Mahadev, the God of Destruction, one of the Trinity, who had granted more lives to the dead than Vishnu.

'When did I do what?'

'Don't you remember Prabhu? Great! You forgot your own good work. That is why you are so great. But at times you should also remember what you have done.'

Vishnu did not understand whether Narad was appreciating him or he was being sarcastic. These journalists often say something and they mean something entirely different. Vishnu remained silent.

'Lord, you are great! But have you really forgotten about Ajamil?'

'Ajamil? Who is that?'

'Remember the *Bhagawata Purana*. Ajamil was a dishonest Brahmin. He committed sins throughout his life. He cheated people. Leaving his children and wife, he used to go to the prostitutes. With age, Ajamil fell ill. His son's name was Narayan. In the end, he called his son all the time: Narayan, Narayan. That way, at the end of his life he took your name. When Yamraj came to take his soul to Mrityuloka, some of you also arrived there to take the soul to Vishnuloka. Yamraj and your guards had a heated argument on where the soul of Ajamil ought to be taken to. Then you arrived there and said that because Ajamil took your name at the end of his life, he will come to Vishnuloka.'

'Yes, I remember now.'

'After this, you became known as *Dayamay*, one who is full of mercy.'

'Yes, now I remember that too.'

'Now, if Yamraj starts doing this, what will happen to your image?'

'What will happen?'

'Your image will be ruined. Prabhu, one's image is a very important aspect of one's identity. Nobody worships any God because of his good work, but because of his image. A lot of research is being undertaken in the world on this subject. I don't have time to talk so much. In short, maintaining the image is important.'

'Hmm...'

'If Yamraj does your job, then why should people worship you? You are one among the Trinity? Will it look good if that Yamraj does what you do? And, he is not even the chief Yamraj, he is the clone of the clone—Yamraj 5003!'

'Hmm. Guess you are right.'

'Think about one more thing. Is granting life something you can do every other day? It should be done only once in a blue moon. Only then people will remember it. You brought one Ajamil to Vishnuloka, but today there are so many people who are named Narayan. Check the voters' list and you will find out. Would you bring all their fathers to Vishnuloka? Now if all Gods and Goddesses start doing this, how will the world run?'

'True. In this manner, the world will cease to function. There will be chaos everywhere,' Vishnu said thoughtfully.

'So, who are you saying this to? You are the Lord of the three worlds. You should formulate the rules and only once in a while should you break the rules.'

'Yes. You are right. Call Yamraj 5003. How dare he spare someone's life like this?'

'Is Yamraj 5003 under my command? Why should he listen to me? You do the needful. My work is to let you know what's happening. Now I will go to Kailash.'

'Why Kailash?'

'I will meet Lord Shiva.'

♣

Shiva was sitting on a flat stone outside his house. He was not in a good mood. Parvati had scolded him in the morning. That was, of course, a good enough reason. Last night, he passed out at the crematorium after smoking weed. Nandi and Bhringi, his attendants, had brought him home. When Shiva gained consciousness in the morning, he discovered himself lying on bed at home. Since then Parvati has been after his life: 'How could someone with a family waste his life like this? Earlier, Kartik and Ganesh were young. Now they have grown up. What impact will all this have on them? What if they start doing the same things?'

What Parvati is saying is not entirely unjustified, but right in the morning? And she is going on and on. No one in the entire universe should get married. How can girls change so much after marriage? When Parvati was meditating hard to get him, was she not aware about his habits? If she knew about it all then, why is she after his life now? Now she says, 'I am turning old. Your children have grown.' How can a God turn old? I am one of the holy Trinity. The moon on my head—does it not signify anything? Moon symbolizes time. It grows and ebbs—it is the symbol of eternity. The world is controlled by time. But Shiva is above the flow of time. That is why the moon is just an ornament for him. Somehow, he has not been able to say all this when Parvati was around. So what if he is a God! Everyone is silenced by his wife.

It has only been a while that Parvati has gone to take a bath. The more he thought about her, her reprimands, the angrier he became. Right at this point, Narad arrived.

'Pranam, Prabhu!'

Seeing Narad, Shiva was not happy at all. He was rather irritated. Whenever this man comes, he brings bad news.

'Bless you, Munivar Narad! You here, at this hour? What news do you bear? Everything well? Or, has there been any problem somewhere?'

'You are right my Lord, it is a very difficult time.'

Mahadev thought, has Narad come to know about Parvati's morning rebuke? If he has, it is bad news indeed. He can keep nothing to himself. Tell him something and the universe will get to know of it the next day.

'Which difficult time are you talking about?'

'You still do not know what has happened?'

'No... I... Actually I was busy the last two days. Which news are you talking about?'

'Your days of power are over. Now you have become powerless.'

Now Mahadev got angry. Narad can never say something directly. He always has a roundabout way of saying things.

'Stop beating around the bush! If you want to tell me something, say it clearly.'

'Yamraj 5003 has given back the life of a dead girl.'

'So? What am I supposed I do?'

'Do you remember Markandya? He was chanting the *Mahamrityunjay Mantra* when he died. You went to bring him to Shivaloka. Yamraj protested. He had said that his soul should go to Yamloka. You refuted him. You said he will come to Shivaloka as he was chanting the Mahamrityunjay Mantra. Yamraj did not listen to you. You killed him, even though you returned his life later. That is why your name is Mahamrityunjay.'

'Yes, I remember. But thousands of years have passed since then.'

'Meanwhile, that Yamraj who you had killed because he refuted you, has become very powerful.'

'That is good!'

'It is good! No wonder your name is "*Bhola*" Maheshwar.'

'What do you mean?'

'You are very forgetful. You don't think about anything. You do not understand what the consequence of an action can be. Someone becoming more powerful than you is an ominous sign.'

'How has Yamraj become more powerful than me?'

'How else? He has started giving people a new lease of life.'

'How is that?'

'So what do you think I have been trying to say for so long? Your days are over. Now even the clones of Yamraj are returning life to the dead. Now, people will worship Yamraj's clones and not you. Nobody will offer you milk.'

As it is Mahadev was angry. He started fuming after listening to all this. He said, 'Okay, is that so? Call Yamraj. I will open my third eye and burn him to ashes. It is not without reason that I am called Trayambakdev. And you know what *Trayambak* means. In my right eye I have the sun, in my left, the moon, and in my third eye I have fire. In this fire, I will burn Yamraj into ashes.'

'Wait! How will you burn Yamraj! Is he Kamadeva, that you will burn him down? He is Yamraj. It is inappropriate to burn him down.'

'What do you mean?'

'You cannot burn Yamraj alone.'

'I cannot burn him alone? Whose assistance do I need?'

'Only the combined strength of Brahma, Vishnu and Maheshwar can burn Yamraj 5003 into ashes. You know Prabhu, these three Gods are not separate. They possess different powers of the same entity. If someone is a doctor, he is also a son, a husband and a father. Similarly, Brahma, Vishnu and Maheshwar are same entities with different roles. They assume different identities to divide the work. The three things needed to run the world are given to them. To create, rear and destroy, are three different roles. Here, destruction is not the end. It is a new beginning. The three powers are seen in the picture of 'Avm'. A denotes Brahma, V denotes Vishnu and M denotes Maheshwar. Without the union of the three, Yamraj cannot be destroyed.'

'Call the two other Gods. Call a meeting of the Trinity. Call Devraj Indra. Call the Chief Yamraj too. We will take a collective decision. Yamraj 5003 should be burnt to death.'

'Beware Prabhu. Never say that you will burn him down!'

'Then?'

'By the term "burning" people understand death. He is already in Yamloka. How can he die? He needs to be stripped of his responsibilities and eventually destroyed.'

'Right. That is exactly what we will do.'

Narahari was a fearless journalist of an Odia daily. A land dealer and the mafia had tried to steal a government plot in Bhubaneswar. Narahari was investigating the story and was murdered midway. When he came to the Mrityuloka, he was told that his sins and good deeds weighed the same. He would have to spend equal number of days in heaven and hell. Narahari said he had heard a lot about hell, so he would like to spend some time there. His guru in journalism had advised him that, as a journalist, it is his duty to find out the truth himself and not to believe anyone. He had heard that things are really painful in hell—the sinners are brutally beaten, whipped, put in boiling oil. But in reality he found that all this no longer happens. Coal is becoming harder and harder to get. Oil has become very expensive in the world and that has had an obvious impact on hell. Hence, the practice of putting the sinners in boiling oil has also been abolished. Yamdoots have become lazy. Beating people up is also a strenuous task. Most of the yamdoots simply do not bother to do that anymore. Then again, some human rights and NGO activists have come to hell. They have complained against the brutal beatings on the inmates of hell to Indra. After this, Chief Yamraj has instructed everyone to be careful. As it is the population of hell has come down drastically in the past few decades—more men and women now to go to heaven. If this trend continues, how will the place run? Therefore, it has been said that if there are too many complaints against a yamdoot, he will be suspended. The food in hell is also not that bad. At least

Narahari gets better food than what he used to during his life as a journalist. He also found out that many of his friends and colleagues are in hell. So, hell is not a bad place as has been indicated by others. He has decided that after a few days, he will take Yamraj's permission and then go to heaven and spend some time there; thereafter he will decide where he would like to settle down.

After staying in hell for a few days, Narahari became friends with some yamdoots. When he was alive, he knew some who have now become yamdoots. When a person meets someone who belongs to the same place as him, it feels excellent—more so, if he comes across him unexpectedly at a distant place. So some of the yamdoots have become friends with Narahari. One of them informed him that there's been a quarrel between Chitragupta and one of the Yamrajs.

Cases of quarrels are not common in the Mrityuloka. Narahari was fast to catch up with the news.

'Chitragupta-Yamraj fight?'

'Not the chief Yamraj, Yamraj 5003.'

'Why?'

'Yamraj 5003 spared the life of young girl.'

'Why did he do that?'

'Yamraj's heart melted as he saw her boyfriend's love for her. He couldn't bear to bring her spirit along.'

'Okay!'

'Old Chitragupta has become furious. He has gone to Brahma to complain. We hear that Yamraj 5003 will be ousted.'

'So he will be suspended?'

'If we use the language of the world, he will be "killed". We don't have death in here, so the ultimate punishment is being burnt with an *agnivaan*. Then, the ashes are kept in a pot and placed over the entrance to hell. There are three reasons for this. First, it will look good. Second, it will be visible to all. And the third reason is that it will act as a warning.'

'Warning?'

'Yes, it will show that if someone defies the norms of Mrityuloka, this is what will happen to him.'

'So will Yamraj 5003 be burnt to ashes?'

'That is what I am waiting to know. But don't tell this to anyone. I have come to know about this from one of Narad's servants.'

Narahari gave word that he would not say anything, but at the end of the day he is a journalist. Till he disseminates a bit of what he has learnt, he cannot rest in peace. And this was no ordinary news. It was big. It had elements of conflict, violence and so much more...

How could he keep it to himself? Within hours, the whole of Mrityuloka was discussing the matter. It is an established fact that the punished usually get all the sympathy. If there is a collision between a cycle and a scooter, it is assumed that the scooter driver is at fault. Similarly, if there is a collision between a scooter and a car, the fault is presumed to be of the car's driver. Again, if there is a collision between a car and a truck, the fault is usually the truck driver's. Finally, the fact that a railway track belongs to the train is ignored when a truck comes on its way at an unmanned railway crossing. Often people blame the train and the signal system and not the truck driver. Now, such sympathy is not pure sympathy; it has an element of pity. Strange are the ways of human psychology.

Anyway, back to the story.

Most of Mrityuloka agreed that Yamraj had done the right thing. How can Yamraj always be so heartless? There have been cases where Gods have shown mercy to mortals in different ways; then where lay the fault with Yamraj 5003? There were some clerks and government officials who said if something happens once, it sets precedence. In government jobs, precedence bears high significance. If a mistake has been committed before, and it has not been pointed out and punishment meted out, it no longer remains a grave mistake. In fact, it often becomes a norm.

Editors of some newspapers and television news channels are also in hell. They are old inhabitants of this place. These days such people, along with the activists, don't usually get to go to hell easily. However, the few editors and social activists who have managed to sneak through, came to know about this and were very excited. 'Is it so? He would be punished without even a trial? We will not let such an injustice happen,' they said.

They went to Devraj Indra together.

'You cannot act this arbitrarily in regard to Yamraj 5003.'

'Action? What action?'

'We know everything. Don't try to cover up.'

'If you know everything, you are bound to agree that Yamraj 5003 has broken the norms of Mrityuloka. He deserves to be punished.'

'How can you say that? How can you mete out a punishment without a fair trial? If at all he has committed a mistake, we need to know how serious it is.'

'In some cases you have to take a quick decision. Else, how can the administration function smoothly?'

'So, does that mean there shall be no justice, no trial? The convict won't be allowed to even defend himself? This is sheer injustice! We will let the people of the world know that such things happen beyond the world. Some of our friends have turned into ghosts and they are living in government offices and secretariats. They will come in the dreams of people and tell everyone what goes on here.'

They continued...

'The entire world will come to know the truth about heaven. The notion that proper justice is always delivered after death will be shattered. People will stop worshipping Gods and Goddesses. Their respect, faith will all bite the dust. Morning and evening they bow before you. That will happen no longer. There shall be no offerings: mothers will stop lighting incense sticks as well. Your photos will now begin to be torn by children and no one will stop them anymore. There shall be no temples on the roadside. Then you will get to see the consequences of such an act.'

Such a barrage of warnings would have alarmed anyone. Indra was no exception. If mortals stop worshipping Gods, what would they be left with? Somehow he managed to camouflage the worry.

'There is nothing that I can do on this matter. The Trinity takes the decision on any action to be taken against a Yamraj.'

'We don't want to know all that. Please inform the Trinity about our intentions. You cannot punish anyone without a fair trial. The accused must get an opportunity to defend himself.'

'How can that happen?'

'What do you mean by "how can that happen"? There should be an open stage. We want to see who says what. If the proceedings of the Indian Parliament can be broadcast live, then why can it not happen here? It is not just the trial of a Yamraj's action. The question is on a policy, the policy followed in heaven. Everyone should know what is happening.'

Alarmed at the increasing protests and the rising voices of the protesters, Indra went to Vishnu and told him everything. Vishnu was taken aback. How has everybody come to know everything? Can nothing stay a secret? Not even in heaven and hell? After analysing the situation, he decided to organize an open trial for Yamraj. Everyone in Devaloka and Mrityuloka would be witness to it. But none from the world need know anything about it.

As Vishnu promised, arrangements were made to broadcast the programme live—to everyone in Devaloka and Mrityuloka. The day arrived and a huge trial courtroom was set up. On the seats of the judges were Brahma, Vishnu and Maheshwar. Along with them were Indra, Chitragupta and the rest on smaller seats. Seated in the front rows were other Gods and Goddesses, along with the other inhabitants of heaven. Also, there was Yami, Yamraj's twin sister. On earth, they call her Yamuna. She is a river there. There are thousands of Yamrajs in Mrityuloka, but every year on the occasion of *bhai dooj*, only Yamraj 5003 visits her. Yami loves this Yamraj. Today is his day of justice. That is why she had come all the way from earth. Narad was also there in the first row.

The trial began.

Vishnu said, 'Friends, you are here at an unprecedented gathering. Never has there been such commotion over the activity of a Yamraj. Chitragupta, tell all of us, what is your complaint against Yamraj 5003?'

Chitragupta stood up from his chair, took out some papers from his small jute bag. He had much to say. The suppressed emotions betrayed the visible calm on his face. He has retained all the invectives Yamraj 5003 had hurled at him for quite some time now. Never before had such a thing happened with him. He had never been insulted in this manner. This was his chance to show Yamraj his position.

Control. Calm down.

He cleared his throat. With his voice smeared in composure, Chitragupta began, 'Yamraj 5003 was assigned the task to bring the soul of a young lady called Sumati

Samanta. He deliberately left it in the world. What is more is that he has given her a new life. She was supposed to be dead.'

Vishnu asked, 'Do you admit this, Yamraj?'

Yamraj: 'Yes, I do. But where is the problem?'

Vishnu: 'Silent. Respond to only what you have been asked.'

Yamraj: 'I have done this.'

Vishnu: 'Chitragupta, continue.'

Chitragupta looked at his papers.

'First, he has broken the norms, the rules, and most importantly, the discipline of Mrityuloka. The universe runs on discipline, not on someone's whims. From sunrise to sunset, ebb and tide, the changing seasons...everything has a rule. Once any system is not complied to, it will become difficult to run the universe. One can spend only that much time in the world as destined. If all Yamrajs start granting life to everyone, does he not take the position of the Almighty?'

'So, what exactly is your allegation?'

'He has done what he is not permitted to do. He has crossed his limit.'

'Yamraj, what do you have to say about this?'

Yamraj 5003 stood up. Everyone's gaze fell upon him. There was a pause. People waited anxiously for his response.

'If doing such a thing has actually harmed the universe in any way, I want to ask if there were any disruptions before when many Gods have done the same. Not only the Gods, even a Yamraj has done such a thing in the past. Have you forgotten Savitri's story? Let me narrate that story. Savitri was the daughter of King Asvapati of the kingdom of Madra. She was sent to select her husband after she attained marriageable age. After passing several kingdoms, she reached a forest. There, she came across King Dyumatsen of the Shalya kingdom. He had lost his kingdom and was in a rather pitiful state. He lived with his wife and son, Satyavan. Satyavan used to gather wood and sell it to earn a living. Savitri chose Satyavan as her husband. Asvapati was not willing to let her daughter get married to poor Satyavan. To add to the trauma, a sadhu professed Satyavan would die within a year. Since he was her first choice, Savitri could not accept anybody else. Asvapati finally gave his assent. A year passed by. Exactly on the day of their first anniversary, Savitri followed Satyavan to the forest. Suddenly, Satyavan started becoming numb. Soon, he lost his ability to stand. He kept his head on her lap and lay down. It was dark everywhere. Yamraj arrived at the spot to take Satyavan's soul. Savitri begged for mercy. Yamraj said, "Nothing can be done. His time is over." Savitri was not going to let Satyavan go so easily. After a while, Yamraj said, "I am very pleased with the kind of love you have for your husband. I will give you a boon. Ask me for anything apart from Satyavan's life." Savitri said, "Then give me a boon, that I may become a mother." Yamraj said, "Amen," and began to take his leave. Savitri started to follow him. Yamraj said, "What happened now?" Savitri replied, "You blessed me with a child. And if you take away my husband, how do I bear a son? Without my husband, how do I become a mother?" Yamraj, not being able to see any way out, had to spare Satyavan's life. Ever since, Savitri has remained an idol. Hundreds of thousands of women do Savitri Vrat in the month of May. Even Yamraj, for that matter, became an idol after this incident. You all know this story. None of you said anything then! In fact, everybody actually appreciated Yamraj's act.

'Now let me tell all of you about Vishnu, the Creator, and Maheshwar, the Destroyer. Even they have let many of their followers have a fresh lease of life. Consider Markandya. He started chanting the Mahamrityunjay Mantra at the time of his death. Yamraj arrived at the scene to take away his soul. But Shiva came down from his abode and asked Yamraj to leave Markandya. When Yamraj declined saying it was against the rule, Lord Shiva killed Yamraj and took Markandya to Shivaloka. It is a separate story that Yamraj was given another birth upon the request of other Gods. Shiva had also burnt Kamadeva, but had to return his life upon the request of Rati, Kamadeva's wife.

'Now see what Vishnu had done. Ajamil was a sinful Brahmin. What did he do? His son's name was Narayan and just because he called his son by the name, which also happened to be the name of Lord Vishnu, he was brought to Vaikunthpuri.

'When the Trinity, the creators do this, there is no harm. Even other Gods have given away lives on a number of occasions. Even a comparatively lesser important Goddess, Manasa, has done this. In Bengal, Bihar, Odisha, Assam, many worship her. In Manasa Mangal, we have the story of Behula-Lakhindar. Lakhindar was the son of Chand Saudagar, who was a wealthy merchant who had many seafaring ships. Chand Saudagar refused to worship Goddess Manasa and she cursed him with the death of Lakhindar through snakebite.

'Lakhindar was married to Behula. Chand Saudagar ordered for a room made of iron. Manasa ordered the builder to keep a hole the size of a needle in it. The night of the marriage, Manasa entered the room in the guise of a snake and bit Lakhindar. Behula woke up and saw her husband was lying dead. Behula did not accept this fate. She said, "I will stay afloat on water with Lakhindar on a boat made from a banana tree." For days Behula prayed and cried. Finally, Manasa returned Lakhindar's life.

'You know this story too. If what I did was wrong, then was that not *wrong*?'

Yamraj 5003 had spoken for quite a while now. Everyone was listening keenly. Everyone looked on. His question reverberated without an answer.

A few minutes of pin-drop silence followed.

After a while, Yamraj 5003 began talking again.

'Savitri and Behula got their husbands Satyavan and Lakhindar. Nobody said anything then. And there is such a massive commotion because I returned Sumati's life seeing Subrata's love for her? When women pray, it is prayer. When a man prays, it is not?'

All the men present in the audience applauded. Yamraj said, 'In this world, only women are entitled to get their husbands back. Men can never get the boon to get back their beloved's life? Isn't this a case of sheer gender bias? In many countries, laws have been made against gender bias. Had you been in the world, you would have been in jail.'

Now, all the women started cheering. One of the activists shouted: 'Anti-women Gods, down, down!'

An elderly activist, Sulochana Devi, who had come to

heaven by virtue of serving women, shouted: 'Sister, these Gods have been oppressing women for ages. They have conspired against us to keep us under men. It is time now to raise our voices against this injustice!'

One of the Gods sitting beside her said, 'Madam, you are wrong. Gods have always shown respect to women.'

'We all know what kind of respect you have shown us. You asked a pious wife like Sita to take a test of fire. Why? Because she was caged in Ravan's Ashokvan for several years, and you thought something immoral may have happened? Good Lord! If Sita was in Ashokvan, imprisoned by Ravan, Lord Ramachandra too was free in the forest. Why no test of fire for him? Whenever Gods fail to contain demons, they will push women to the forefront. Go fight! Who will kill Mahishasura? Durga. Who can kill Raktabija? Kali. At that time they will praise the women like anything. They will call her Shaktirupa, Brahmaswarupa. But each time there is a demand for giving women equal rights as men, you all tactfully avoid the issue. We will not let such discrimination continue any longer. Say, sisters: "Anti-women Gods! Down, down!"'

The words were repeated a few times: 'Anti-women Gods, down, down!'

Vishnu noticed that the situation was slowly going out

of control. He said, 'Madam, you do have a logic in what you are saying. But this is not the right place to discuss all this. Please don't forget that we have gathered here to discuss an important issue. Please do not waste our time this way. Come to Vishnuloka later, we can discuss the matter with you there at length then.'

Sulochana Devi returned to her seat. Very few people get the opportunity to go to Vishnuloka. She was happy to have received an invitation.

Vishnu said, 'See, Yamraj 5003, I do agree that you have a point. But just imagine if all the Gods gave back lives, what would the state of the world be?'

'Prabhu, should there not be one rule for everyone? One rule for one god, another rule for another? If such discrimination remains in heaven, how can you rule the entire universe? Because of such discrimination, demons rise in rebellion from time to time. And, always, instead of setting things right at your end, you have portrayed them in a bad light. Their genuine grievances have never been addressed.'

Vishnu said, 'Now you are switching to another topic, Yamraj. Stick to the subject.'

'You are not letting me speak. This also a kind of suppression.'

'Suppression?'

'Yes. Just think, my Lord, the kind of suppression and injustice you have meted out to me. What I was, and look, what I have become today. The Sun God is my father. My mother is Sanjana. Some say Shani is my brother. Yami and I are twins. We were the first human beings to be sent to earth. The Vedas say I was the first person who came to Mrityuloka. You asked me to become its master. I was so happy then. You gave me the honour of a Dharmaraj, the King of Dharma—righteousness. You said it was my responsibility to maintain dharma throughout the world. First you made me the king of righteousness, and then you made me the God of Mrityuloka. You announced that Yamraj was the God of the south end of the world, which is considered to be the lowland. Then, you presented me to everyone as a cruel and brutal figure. You gave me a black buffalo as my companion. You changed my colour to green. You gave me an unusually thick and awkward moustache. You handed me a rope and a mace. At times I have also been portrayed as someone with the head of a bull. Today, I have to drag the souls of human beings to Mrityuloka, then analyse their deeds and finally ensure that they get what they deserve.'

He paused for a while, took a deep breath, and continued.

'You painted such a horrific picture of mine, my Lord.

You described me as the lord of hundreds of diseases. Just think Prabhu, what a terrible image you created of me! In a way, you equated dharma with fear. Dharma should have been about happiness and love. People should have embraced dharma as a part of their lives. How could you attach that with fear, Prabhu? And then somehow dharma became a synonym for religion. People will follow the path of religion, just out of fear? This is how you pushed men away from the real spirit of dharma. It is no longer something dear. You did not understand the simple thing that if you wanted to induce religion into the hearts and souls of people, you should have followed the path of love, not fear. Just for your advantage, you sort of ethically handicapped the human race.'

Another brief silence followed.

'You were not satisfied by portraying me in such a light in the Hindu shastras. Even in Buddhism, you presented me in the same light. At first, my identity was negated in Buddhism. It was said man would get rewards or sufferings in his next birth, so there was absolutely no need of someone who will judge the sins and good deeds. Chitragupta lost his job. Then, I returned again, but my picture remained the same—as dangerous as it had been. I became the Lord of *Patal*, the underworld. In certain Buddhist scriptures, Yamraj was portrayed as Mara who tried to distract Buddha during his meditation under the Bodhi tree. Later, Buddhism got divided into two sections—Bajrajan or Mahajan, and Hinjaan. Bajrajan and Tibetan Buddhisim continued to portray a frightening image of mine. A mirror in the left hand—the reflector of karma—and a sword of justice in the right. In Japanese Buddhism, I was called Yamma. The picture was of someone who judges one after death. I have always been portrayed as a god of fear. Why, my Lord? Am I really that dangerous? Was there any need to make me so fearsome? You know that without me the universe cannot run. Without death, life cannot continue. But none of you presented my contribution in the correct way. You are part of the holy Trinity. Such injustice to someone is unbecoming of you.'

Vishnu saw the discussion was taking a totally new turn.

'Yamraj, we have gathered here to discuss something specific. You have given life back to a girl unlawfully. Do not waste our time by discussing other issues.'

Yamraj 5003 said, 'I have nothing more to say.'

'You still do not think that you have committed a mistake by giving Sumati a new life?'

'No, I have done no wrong.'

'Do you repent in anyway? You can tell me without any hesitation.'

'I just said. I have done no wrong. I did what my heart said. You can never be wrong when you follow your heart, especially when the act does good to someone. Since I did no wrong, the question of repentance does not arise. You can do as you please.'

Vishnu started addressing the audience, 'We have heard the accusations against Yamraj 5003, and we have also heard his defence. Next, we, the Trinity, will decide the course of action. The meeting is over. We will let you know our decision.'

Brahma, Vishnu and Maheshwar had a closed-door meeting in the evening for quite some time. The Trinity decided to destroy Yamraj 5003. They decided that his body would be burnt down with agnivaan.

Brahma said, 'We will not keep the ashes of Yamraj 5003 in the golden urn, as is the norm in heaven. We will spread it across the seven seas.

'Why?' asked Mahadev.

'So that another life is not born out of the ashes. We do not want such a Yamraj to return again.'

'You are right, Prajapita. If this Yamraj remains, or gets a new life, he will continue to disrupt the functioning of the universe. The Yamraj has a strange softness. If we allow such a Yamraj, the working of the universe is bound to get affected adversely. Each position is associated with some responsibility. The higher the position, the bigger the responsibility. If someone cannot do his work, he ought to be removed,' said Vishnu.

'You are right, Vishnu. First responsibility and then discipline. Emotions should come later.'

Maheshwar said that the act of burning down Yamraj 5003 has to be carried out secretly. Brahma agreed. 'The sympathy of everyone present in the gathering is with Yamraj 5003. He has everyone's support. If they come to know that he is being destroyed forever, there shall be a public furore.'

Maheshwar was thinking. 'How should we do this?'

Wrinkles of worry appeared on Brahma's four foreheads.

Vishnu thought for a while. 'Let's do this. First we will announce that Yamraj 5003 has fallen ill, his brain is showing signs of decay. Then, you say that during his creation, there were some problems in his brain. If people want to know the problem and its details, say something that makes sense. But say it in such a way that is not understandable to those present at the meeting. What needs to be said, I am sure you would know better.'

'Right.'

'Then after few more days, say Yamraj 5003 is in a very critical condition. His behaviour is showing serious abnormalities. It is to his advantage that the Yamraj is being taken away from his work. If you say it step by step in this manner, it will not astonish anyone. The job will be done peacefully.'

Mahadev said, 'Sadhu Sadhu! Here comes your intelligence. Maheshwar gives thee a million salutes. You found out such a simple solution to such a complex issue.'

'Wait. Don't be so happy right away. Let the job be done first!'

nine

And Finally...

Sumati and Subrata are happily living together.

After returning from hospital, Subrata and Sumati got back to each other. Initially, Sumati was not ready to marry Subrata. She had said, 'I am no longer worthy of you...'

'How can you say such a thing? I love you, dear!'

'You don't know all that's happened with me. I have been violated...'

'I know that, dear.'

'You know?'

'Yes, I know everything. I have heard about it.'

'Who told you all this?'

'You.'

'Me? When?'

'When you were in a state between consciousness and semi-consciousness.'

'And still you want to marry me?'

'Yes, I still want to marry you. Because I always loved you. I never loved your body, Sumati. I loved you. Sanctity lies in the mind, in the soul, not in the body.'

'But what else is left in this life?'

'What do you mean by "this life" Sumati? Do you know you have been blessed with a rebirth? Consider everything as an accident and move on. Let's start our life afresh.'

It was not easy to forget everything, but Sumati somehow managed to do so. As the years passed, she began forgetting her gory past. She started forgetting all that had transpired as a horrible nightmare. She has found her man in Subrata, her dream man. She is trying to enjoy her life to the fullest. She has lost a lot of time. But what is done cannot be undone. The past cannot return. What can be done is making the most of the life ahead. Today, she realizes the small pleasures of life. Today, she experiences the beauty of life. She never thought that even stitching the buttons on Subrata's clothes and cooking food for him could be so beautiful. The dreams of being a leading heroine was a nightmare long gone. At times, she smiles when she thinks that her dreams were so...

Subrata never told Sumati that Yamraj had given her a new life. Even Sumati never felt that any such thing had happened with her. In fact, at times Subrata doubts if it actually happened. People hallucinate during times of crisis. Yamraj's coming, tying of Sumati's soul with a rope, the conversation Subrata then had with him, and finally Yamraj sparing her life...could all this be true?

In a special room in Brahmaloka, Yamraj 5003 is lying on an ivory bed. Somehow, he is not being able to sleep. He is sad and lost. It is only yesterday that he has been told that while he was made, there were some problems. Now the problems have become serious. Therefore, in the larger interest of the Mrityuloka, he will be debarred from service. He knows the significance of being 'debarred'. His body will be destroyed. He has understood why his body will be destroyed. He has questioned the authority of the Trinity. He has given back the life of someone who was destined to die. Despite being a Yamraj, he is sentimental, he is emotional, he has empathy. That is unbecoming of him or any of his clones. No, he did not fear death. He has been seeing death very closely. No anger, no fear or no deep sadness; there is only a feeling of being lost. Can he not have some sentiments? So what if he is a Yamraj?

Suddenly, Yamraj 5003 remembered the couple—

Subrata and Sumati. How would they be doing now? Ah! Let them be well. Let them live happily. Let them live with love. Let love live. He gathered all his blessings and wished them happiness.

Brahma, Vishnu and Maheshwar chanted their mantras and activated the agnivaan, the arrow which would spew fire. It travelled at great speed and pierced into the heart of Yamraj 5003. His body started burning. While burning, Yamraj addressed the Trinity, 'Prabhu, you have destroyed me, but remember, in the cleave of a stone, grass shall come and a flower will be born. However hard the stone might be, it shall see the birth of a flower. There shall exist acts of kindness and forgiveness. Till the universe lives, these feelings shall remain. Despite my destruction. Amen...'

Within moments, his body turned into ashes. Till the last moment there remained a strange expression of serenity on his face. Only when someone considers his life to be successful can such an expression be seen at the time of his destruction.

The Trinity gathered the ashes in a golden urn. Then they sat on Garuda, the animal-bird, Vishnu's carrier, and from the heavens they sprinkled the ashes into the seven seas. They were soon lost. The Trinity returned to their respective abodes.

❧

In Brahmaloka, Brahma said to Saraswati, 'I am very sad today. Yamraj 5003 was probably right. Without love, kindness, sympathy and compassion, what meaning will our creation have?'

❧

After Vishnu returned to Vishnuloka, Lakshmi said, 'You have come at the right time. Just see how I am looking in this saree. I got it from the world only today. The weavers have done a great job. Look how beautiful this saree is…'

Vishnu said, 'Lakshmi, I just want to spend some time alone.'

'What is wrong, my Lord?'

'It's a long story Lakshmi. Just know that today I have yet again understood how difficult it is to be a preserver. On so many occasions, there is a direct conflict between the heart and the head and we have to take a hard decision. Let me be alone, for a while.'

❧

In Kailash, Mahadev asked Parvati for some weed to smoke.

'Again?'

Parvati would have said more, but seeing Maheshwar's expression, she just handed over the grass and left him alone.

Narad is quite happy. Yamraj 5003 has finally been destroyed. But why this sense of something incomplete? Is it not the real happiness? Why is it that his eyes are turning moist? Why does he feel like crying? Why can he not look into the mirror? He should be happy. Is he?

The seas gladly accepted the ashes of Yamraj Number 5003. However, only one tiny particle swam across and reached a coast and found soft, moist and warm soil.

And then…

What happened after this, is another story.

Glossary

agnivaan The arrow that spews fire

bahan carrier

Bhagawata Purana It is one of Hinduism's eighteen great *Puranas*, or ancient sacred texts. It is a revered text in Vaishnavism, a Hindu tradition that reveres Lord Vishnu.

Bhai dooj It is a festival celebrated by Hindus of India and Nepal on the second lunar day of Shukla Paksha (bright lunar fortnight) in the Hindu calendar month of Kartik. The celebrations of this day are similar to the festival of Raksha Bandhan. On this day, sisters pray for the long life of their brothers and get gifts from brothers.

Brahmaloka In Hinduism, Brahmaloka or Brahmapura is the abode of Brahma, one of the three Trimurti (holy Trinity).

Dayamay One full of mercy

Devraj Lord of the Gods

Dhenki It is an old-style rice mill found in the East Indian states of Assam, West Bengal, Odisha, parts of Bihar and also in Bangladesh. Such tools have been used in Japan too. It is usually made of hard wood. It has a fulcrum supporting a weight. Due to the force of the weight upon the rice in the pods, the rice and the golden brown husks separate. Dhenki was usually operated by women to produce rice from paddy and grind rice to powder. Legend has it that this used to be the carrier of Narad. He used to roam all three lokas riding on his dhenki.

Devaloka The abode of the Gods

Gandharva A name used for distinct heavenly beings in Hinduism and Buddhism. In Hinduism, Gandharvas are believed to be good-looking and are skilled singers and dancers.

gupt Secret; secrecy

Kamadeva The God of Love. Kamadeva was assigned with the mission to stop Lord Shiva's penance that he started after the death of Sati Devi. Advised by Brahma, Kamadeva tried to stop the penance by creating sexual desire and passion in Lord Shiva. Shiva's meditation was interrupted and he was terribly angry and opened his third eye on his forehead, and a fierce blazing flame came out of his third eye and burned Kamadeva into ashes.

kaya Body

Mahamrityunjay Mantra It is also called the *Rudra Mantra*, referring to the furious aspect of Lord Shiva; the *Trayambakam Mantra*, alluding to Shiva's three eyes; and sometimes known as the *Mritasanjivini Mantra* because it is a component of the 'life-restoring' practice given to the primordial sage Sukracharya after he had completed an exhausting period of austerity. It is addressed to Rudra or Lord Shiva in his fiercest and most destructive *roopa* or feature.

manas santan One who is not a biological son but considered as close as a son

manaspat The mind

Mrityuloka The abode of the Dead

Munivar A form of address for a sage

Panji (or Panchang) Panchang is Vedic almanac—an ancient Vedic calendar in a tabulated form that helps to know the auspicious and inauspicious time. People use it extensively to fix dates for marriages and other ceremonies. In Odisha and Bengal, traditionally panjis are printed on low-cost paper with many pictures of Gods and Goddesses including the picture of the Goddess Kali.

Patal The mythical underworld. It is believed that there are three lokas: *swarg*, the heaven, inhabited by the Gods; *martya*, the Earth, inhabited by the human beings; and patal, the underworld, inhabited by the demons.

Prabhu God

pranam Obeisance

punya What one earns as a result of indulging in virtuous deeds.

Rambha In Hindu mythology, Rambha is the queen of the *apsara*s, the magical and beautiful female beings in Devaloka. She is unrivalled in her accomplishments in the arts of dance and music, and beauty. She is often asked by the king of the Devas, Indra, to break the tapasya of sages so that the purity of their penance is tested against temptation, and also that the order of the three worlds remains undisturbed by any one man's mystical powers.

rasa A rasa (which literary means 'juice' or 'essence') denotes an essential mental state and is the dominant emotional theme of a work of art or the primary feeling that is evoked in the person that views, reads or hears such a work. Bharata Muni enunciated the eight rasas in the *Natyashastra*, an ancient work of dramatic theory. Later, a ninth rasa was accepted after an extended philosophical and aesthetic theorization by Abhinavagupta, and the expression *Navarasa* (the nine rasas) could come into vogue.

Savitri vrat An occasion where married women observe a fast praying for the long life of their husbands.

somras Divine liquor

Vishnuloka The abode of Vishnu, one of the holy Trinity.

yamdoot *Doot* literally means messenger. Yamdoot means messenger of Yam—strong-bodied beings who accompany Yamraj in bringing the souls to Mrityuloka.

yoni A stylized representation of the female genitalia representing the goddess Shakti in Hinduism. It also means 'species'.